Dear Mystery Reader:

Marian Babson has been delighting mystery readers for years with her wonderful cat cozies. PAWS FOR ALARM is the latest installment in her utterly purrfect cat series.

If you haven't discovered Marian's mysteries yet, you're in for a real treat. Like Lillian Jackson Brown and Carole Nelson Douglas, Marian is a master of feline suspense. This time out, the Harper family does a summer swap, leaving their New England home for a cozy cottage in a village just outside of London. The Harpers' new home is oh so cozy, and even comes with a shy marmalade cat named Esmond. But life isn't all tea and crumpets for the visiting family; someone's trying to kill Mr. Harper! With the genteel village turning awfully sinister, the Harpers may find that their adopted orange cat may hold all the answers.

I know you'll enjoy Marian's latest mystery, but be warned, those adorable paw prints may just lead to murder!

Yours in crime,

Joe Veltre

Joe Veltre
Assistant Editor
St. Martin's Press DEAD LETTER Paperback Mysteries

WHAT THE CAT DRAGGED IN. . .

My husband had been in London all day. He'd warned me that he might be a bit late as there were a couple of bookstores in Charing Cross Road he wanted to visit. I knew Arnold when he got in a bookstore—he looked on them as libraries with price tags—he was almost impossible to dislodge until the place closed for the night.

So I wasn't surprised at how late he was. Annoyed, but not surprised.

I turned the oven on its lowest setting and worked off my irritation by whipping cream with a manual eggbeater. When the doorbell rang—just like him to forget his key again—I ignored it. I heard the twins' footsteps racing for the door. Then:

"Hey, Mom—" Donald shouted gleefully. "Guess what? Dad's under arrest!"

I dropped the eggbeater on the table and it rolled to the floor, scattering dollops of cream all the way. I was vaguely aware of a delighted Esmond advancing upon this unexpected largesse as I dashed for the front door.

I took one look at Arnold—held upright by a policeman on either side of him—and screamed.

Paws
for
Alarm

Marian Babson

St. Martin's Paperbacks

First published in Great Britain by Collins Crime, an imprint of HarperCollins *Publishers*, as *Death Swap*.

PAWS FOR ALARM

Library of Congress Catalog Card Number: 97-16232

ISBN: 0-312-96513-3

Printed in the United States of America

St. Martin's Paperbacks edition/May 1998

St. Martin's Paperbacks are published by St. Martin's Press, 175 Fifth Avenue, New York, NY 10010.

10 9 8 7 6 5 4 3 2 1

Paws
for
Alarm

One

We had flown out from Logan Airport in the middle of a scorcher that showed no sign of abating. When it gets that hot so early in the summer, it usually means we're in for a blistering heat wave that can go on for weeks. What New England would be like in the August Dog Days didn't bear thinking about.

We landed at Heathrow and stepped out into a blissful, cool dampness; more mist than rain, really. I felt my drooping spirits begin to revive like a parched plant suddenly watered and moved to a shady spot.

'It's raining!' Arnold was prepared to make a production out of it. He threw back his shoulders as much as the suitcases he was carrying allowed and looked upwards into the mist. 'The same rain that fell on Disraeli, on Palmerston, on –'

'Not quite the same, dear.' If I didn't bring him down to earth occasionally, I had the uneasy feeling that he might float away someday – leaving us behind. Of course, there were also moments – like now – when I felt I'd like to help the process along by giving him a kick that would blast him through the fourth dimension and into his dear Queen Victoria's Court. 'It's been recycled a few hundred thousand times since then.'

'Never mind that,' Arnold persisted stubbornly.

'It's liquid history, drifting down on us, enveloping us –'

'I'm getting wet,' Donna said.

'So am I,' Donald chimed in. They both levelled accusing eyes on their father.

Young as the twins were, they somehow realized the perilous hold their father had on reality and the twentieth century; like me, they were afraid that he might slip away into that earlier era if we relaxed our vigilance. Especially now that he had the summer in which to roam through the century of his heart's delight, in the country where he not-so-secretly felt he should have been born.

'All right, all right,' Arnold sighed. He gave one final upward glance, calling upon something beyond our ken to witness how crudely his aspirations were treated; promising another, deeper, communion once he had got these dreeadful incubi settled and off his mind. 'Where's the car park?'

'That's immaterial,' I said. 'We only get the house, don't you remember? The car was totalled in that accident.'

'I thought you made arrangements to have one hired and waiting for us.'

'Oh, no, dear, that was your responsibility. I arranged the house swap, organized the packing, gave our own house the most thorough cleaning it's ever known, handled the correspondence, got the children ready . . . That was the one little detail *you* were supposed to take care of. Do you mean you didn't?'

The question was rhetorical. We walked on in silence. I'd suspected Arnold hadn't done a thing about the car hire, but I'd been too annoyed to

8

remind him. Let him bury himself in his files, his reference books and his research – the time was coming when he would have to face the real world. And he was going to do it the hard way, without the supporting infrastructure of academia, without a secretary, without his clubs and cronies – and without any cooperation from me.

I hadn't wanted to come. I'd been stretching the truth when I said I'd arranged the house swap. I hadn't. Celia had.

'There's a sign for a bus going into London over there.' Donald pointed and I didn't bother to reprimand him.

'And a Tube station – ' Donna pointed, too. 'Can we go by Tube, please, can we?'

'May we?' Arnold corrected absently, veering in the indicated direction.

I followed along, still brooding. I shouldn't be here at a time like this, a time when my cousin and best friend, Patrick, was on the verge of a breakdown and needed me. It could be argued that Arnold and the kids needed me, too, but sometimes I doubted it. I knew for a fact that Patrick needed all the affection and moral support he could gather about him right now. I had been prepared to give it to him.

That was why Celia had sent me away.

Oh, not overtly – she was too clever for that. She had begun by working on Arnold, telling him how valuable it would be if he could spend the summer in England researching primary sources. She got him to agree that as little as three months direct research would be of immense value to his work. Once planted, the seed sprouted beyond all recognition in just a few days. Only the mechanics – and the expense – held him back.

Then Celia revealed that her recently-widowed sister, Rosemary Blake, would like to come over to the States for a few months to escape unhappy memories and recover a bit from her bereavement. What could be easier – and more convenient – than a house swap?

'We'll be democratic about this – ' Arnold halted at the entrance to the public transport system. 'Who wants to go by bus and who votes for the Tube?'

I looked away, abstaining from the vote. Celia had never been able to grasp the essential relationship between Patrick and me. She had always been jealous of me.

The twins had a brisk argument. Donald favoured the bus, Donna the Tube. Arnold heard someone say that the Tube was faster and that decided it. He wanted to get everything over as quickly as possible and disappear into his musty old manuscripts.

'Where do we want to go?' Arnold asked, squinting at the Tube map. I ignored the question and he got into the line for the ticket office.

Ideal,' Celia had said. '*It would be ideal.*' Her sister had a house – well, a semidetached – within easy striking distance of London and all its research libraries and museums, and we had a house by the lake in New Hampshire, very near Celia's. Why didn't we just do a house swap, as so many were doing these days? Arnold could do his research in England and Celia's newly-widowed sister could be near her for this difficult summer. '*You even –* ' Celia had said it as though presenting an instance of Divine

Intention – 'both have cats. So you'd feel at home and you wouldn't have to worry about who was going to look after the cat!'

I took this with a grain of salt – in Errol's case, it was every cat for himself – but Arnold lapped it up. He'd been more than halfway convinced ever since Celia had first broached the subject. A summer in England – rent-free – who could ask for anything more?

I could, but my wishes weren't considered.

'Come on – ' Arnold waved tickets at me. 'This way!'

We plunged into the maelstrom of red-eyed, wearied travellers heading for the trains. They were shouting to each other in a dozen different languages, most of which I had never heard before. Suitcases bumped into the back of my legs, nearly knocking me off my feet. As I staggered, I was buffeted by backpacks and got more elbows in my ribs pushing me out of the way than helping hands extended to steady me. Donna got a clout on the head from a carelessly-handled duffel bag and began to cry.

'Arnold,' I said, 'couldn't we at least have taken a taxi?'

'Too late,' he shouted back cheerfully. 'We've got the tickets now. Not much further,' he encouraged Donna. 'Just ahead, see?'

We gained the station platform and were able to set down our suitcases, forming ourselves into a defensive group. We must have looked like an Old West wagon train drawn into a circle against the attacking Redskins.

There was a roar in the distance, a rush of high

wind down the tunnel and the train charged into the station. A door opened right in front of us and we just had time to pick up our cases before we were caught in the forward surge.

'Where are all those orderly queues we used to hear about?' I gasped as we fell into seats and fought to keep our luggage clear of some swarthy men who seemed to want to kick it to the far end of the car.

'We'll probably find them farther into the country,' Arnold said encouragingly. 'Once we get away from all these foreigners.'

We were foreigners, too. I knew the thought had never occurred to Arnold. In his own mind, hobnobbing with the phantoms of his historical period, he was probably the equal, if not the superior, of anyone in England short of the Royal Family – and I wouldn't be too sure about them. When Arnold's imagination got going . . .

Celia had played on it like a lute. It would be *so* different from arriving in a country and staying at a hotel; we would walk into a fully-equipped home; walk into a circle of friends and neighbours who would welcome us for Rosemary's sake; we would live like the English themselves. How much nicer than taking our chances in any squalid rented accommodation. The best part was that it would be free, and we could use all those extra savings to travel around and see the country – perhaps even some of the Continent.

When I demurred, I was a spoilsport. Even the twins had succumbed to the spell Celia had woven. Worst of all, I couldn't come out with the truth: they would refuse to believe it.

Celia was doing all this to get rid of me. Oh, she was happy enough to do Arnold a good turn but, basically, she was doing it to get me out of the country – far, far away, for a nice indefinite period. Probably she hoped we'd never come back; at least, that I wouldn't.

She had never been able to understand that Patrick and I were best friends, as well as cousins – but nothing more. She was consumed by the kind of jealousy that fuelled old Greek legends. Whenever she watched us together, even chaperoned by our respective progeny, she suspected the worst. She hid it fairly well from the others, but there was always the barb beneath the surface when she spoke to me. It was totally unfair, but I could never convince her of the innocence of our relationship. Perhaps part of her problem was that she was from another country and her childhood memories took another frame of reference. Whenever Patrick and I referred to our shared childhood and common memories, she broke out in a seething rash.

Just let me catch Patrick's eye and say, '*Who knows what evil lurks in the heart of a man?*' and Patrick lift his arm to eye level, raising an imaginary cloak of invisibility and reply, '*The Shadow knows . . . heh . . . heh*' and Celia would go up in flames. It got so bad I didn't dare even remark, '*Gee willikins, Daddy Warbucks!*' or use any other catch phrases from the childhood wealth that social historians had now solemnized as Popular Culture.

I tried to tell myself that Celia was just insecure, but every now and again I was swamped by a rage to match her own – nobody needed to be that insecure!

She was cutting Patrick and me off from our past, driving us apart. She wanted to be the one and only female in his life. It was just as well she'd produced a son, rather than a daughter who wouldn't have stood a chance either.

Now that Patrick was ill, it was even worse. They were calling it Executive Burn-out, which was as good a name as any for the old-fashioned nervous breakdown threatening because his business was teetering on the edge of failure due to the recession. Apart from financial support, he needed moral support, reassurance, friends around him; I could have been a stabilizing presence, but Celia had succeeded in getting rid of me. She wanted to be Patrick's main support and now she was.

Poor Patrick. Celia herself had always struck me as a nervous breakdown looking for a place to happen. She was too tall, too thin, quivering with nerves like an overbred horse. She would not be a soothing influence at a time like this.

I had tried to like her. I liked her well enough. We would never be bosom buddies, but we might have been slightly better friends if she hadn't distrusted me so.

Now she had banished me to the strange territory she had come from. In nightmares just before our departure, I had dreamed of myself surrounded by thousands of Celia clones, all quivering with nerves, neighing disapproval and hating me.

I wasn't looking forward to several months in their company.

* * *

The train lurched to a halt and shut off power, the carriage shivered violently, then went still. All around us backpackers sprang into action, leaping from their seats and struggling to reshoulder their burdens.

'Come on.' Arnold got to his feet. 'This is our stop.'

Once again we battled our way on to an almost perpendicular escalator, grimly clutching luggage and children. Strange advertising messages on small upright posters kept the twins busy reading all the way to the surface. I was glad someone was amused; I was getting a headache.

We negotiated a passageway, then a couple of flights of stairs and emerged into a grubby run-down area that looked more like a combat zone than a glamorous introduction to one of the world's most historic and cultural cities.

'Arnold, are you sure we're in the right place?'

'Of course I am.' He took a better grip on the suitcases and looked around dubiously.

'There's a penny arcade!' Donald shouted rapturously. 'Can we go in? Just for a minute? Can we go in?'

'NO!' His father and I thundered in chorus, unanimous for once. The place looked like some murky depth of an unsavoury ocean – and as for the denizens swimming around just behind the dark plate glass windows . . . well!

'Arnold, what are we doing here? I mean, why did you get tickets to this place? I've never heard of it and – ' I broke off as a girl with a shaven head, except for two long thin braids, drifted past us and entered the penny arcade.

'Somebody told me it was a good place to – '

Arnold's voice faded as the vision walked past him and his head turned automatically to follow her progress. 'I mean – ' He cleared his throat and got a fresh grip on himself as well as the cases. 'They said there were cheap hotels here and – '

This time two boys with orange, green and purple hair radiating in spikes from their scalps came along. They were too busy holding hands to notice us, but we sure noticed them.

'Wow!' Donald said. 'Did you see that hair?'

'Don't stare,' I said automatically. 'Arnold, do you know where we're going? I'm sure these aren't the directions Celia gave us.'

'We'll go there later,' Arnold said firmly. 'Maybe tomorrow. I thought, today, we could stay at a hotel in the city and you and the kids could get acclimatized while I found the London Library and asked about joining. Come on – ' He turned in the direction of a leafy square just off the main drag – and I was beginning to suspect that drag was the right word.

'Arnold, I'd rather go straight to the house and start getting acclimatized there.' We followed him uncertainly. He was nowhere near as confident as he was pretending to be.

The square was bordered with small hotels. It was also lined with females, either standing alone or in clusters of two or three. They watched us with speculative eyes as we walked along, innocently reading out the names of hotels to each other.

My first reaction was a rather relieved thought that I was not going to be surrounded by Celia-clones in this country, after all. None of these women looked like Celia. This was rapidly followed by an unnerving second thought: they looked like . . .

'Arnold – ' I said. 'Arnold, we're not staying here!'

'I guess maybe it's not such a good idea,' he agreed uneasily. 'Maybe we ought to try another part of town – '

'Maybe we ought to go straight to Waterloo Station and take the train to St Anselm, the way we're supposed to!'

'Well . . .' With a deep sigh, Arnold turned slowly and began leading us back to King's Cross Station. 'There's a subway line to Waterloo – '

'No, Arnold.' I put my foot down. 'This time we're taking a taxi.'

Two

'Is this the place?' Donald asked incredulously.

'This is it.' Surreptitiously, I checked the address again, just to be sure. The house lurking behind the tall holly hedge was smaller than it had appeared in the photographs Celia had shown us and, although we had known it was semi-detached, somehow the other half of the house seemed to impinge more.

'It's teensy,' Donna said. 'Our house is a lot bigger.'

'All houses are different.' Arnold was impatient. He had paused at the station to collect a timetable. Already, in his mind, he was halfway to the London Library, the Reading Room of the British Museum, the Library in the Houses of Parliament. It was a great trial to him that he had to see his family settled before he was off about his precious research. It was martyrdom that the process was taking so long that he could not possibly get back to London before all the libraries closed for the day.

'We didn't exchange on a room-for-room basis,' he explained. 'We exchanged for the privilege of residing as natives in another country; of moving into an existing circle of friends and being treated as one of them; of – '

'Enough – ' I cut him short. 'Let's go inside and view the damage.'

You had to hand it to Celia. When she sold a sucker on an idea, they stayed sold.

Once inside, we discovered the house was bigger than it looked. It would have to be. The rooms were spacious and the building made up in length what it lacked in breadth. I was relieved to see that the long wide downstairs hallway ran along the inner side, against the other half of the house. From the position of the two front doors, I assumed that the Sandgates' hallway ran parallel, for which I was duly grateful. The kids can get noisy at times and that would cut down the nuisance factor. We'd never lived in such close proximity to other people before; I was not at all sure how it was going to work out.

'Well . . .' Arnold set down the suitcases and looked around. 'Well . . . this is fine. Just fine . . . great . . .' He looked at his watch and shook his head sadly. I could see the thought moving through his mind as clearly as if it had been flashing across his forehead in neon lights: *An early night and the first train in the morning back to London and the libraries.*

'Well,' Arnold said brightly as though the idea had just occurred to him, 'why don't we get to bed and we can get off to a good start bright and early in the morning?'

'We can't go to bed now,' Donald said indignantly. 'It's still light out.'

'That's right,' I agreed. 'Furthermore, it's only eleven o'clock in the morning back home. We may be jet-lagged, but our interior clocks are going to take a few days to adjust. We're wide awake, even if we are exhausted. Apart from which, we want to do some shopping. *Food* shopping – ' I cut Arnold off in mid-wince. 'We don't know what sort of emergency provisions Rosemary may have left for us.' If she was anything like Celia, I was prepared to mistrust any arrangements she might have made.

'That's a thought. Why don't we go and look?' When you got on to the subject of food, you hit Arnold where he lived. He headed in the probable direction of the kitchen with nearly as much animation as if it were a reference library. The rest of us trailed after him.

It was an ordinary kitchen, and yet there was something different about it. I stood in the doorway trying to spot the difference while Arnold strode straight to the refrigerator, threw open the door and stooped to examine the contents. The twins crowded behind him.

'There's a lot of cream in here,' Arnold reported over his shoulder. 'Someone must think Americans live on coffee and cream.'

'It isn't cream – ' Donna had snatched up one of the small cartons and was reading the information printed on it. 'It's milk! Those dinky little things are what they put the milk in!' She whooped with laughter. 'Donald can drink more than that all by himself.'

'The eggs are smaller, too,' Donald said accusingly.

'Everything is smaller here.' I had recognized the major difference about the kitchen; the minor one was that everything appeared to be about ten years behind the times, although obviously fairly new. 'We'll get used to it. Meanwhile, I suggest we go into town and get something to eat there, because I sure as hell am not going to do any cooking tonight.'

'Sure, honey, sure,' Arnold said quickly, recognizing the dangerous note in my voice. 'We didn't mean to imply that you should. We were just looking to see what was around. We'll go get a real English meal, then we'll find a supermarket and pick up some groceries, and then – ' a major concession – 'we'll get a taxi back here.'

By the time we got back, I was in a worse mood. My feet were wet, my head was aching and my stomach had begun a pitched battle with the food I had just sent down to it. To make matters worse, the twins had reached the whining stage.

'I didn't come three thousand miles,' I complained, while Arnold fumbled for the key, 'to eat hamburgers and French fries in a fast food outlet that would have been closed down by any right-thinking Board of Health in the States.'

'They were pretty funny-tasting hamburgers,' Donald said.

'That's because they were half lamb,' I said. 'Or maybe fat pork. And those French fries were almost solid lumps of grease – and stale grease, at that.'

'Mom, I think I'm going to be sick.' Donna had turned an unhealthy colour and was breathing heavily through her mouth.

'Be reasonable, Nancy – ' Arnold was getting his beleaguered look. 'It was the only place open. You saw that for yourself. What else could we do?'

'And that's another thing. Who ever heard of half-day closing? Shutting up everything at one o'clock in the middle of the week? Even the taxis disappeared!'

'All right, all right,' Arnold said. 'I'll hire a car first thing in the morning.'

'Damn right, you will!' So far as I was concerned, the gloves were off. 'Are they all crazy over here?'

'Shhh!' Arnold looked around nervously as my voice rose. It was true that several people had suddenly appeared on the street, but they appeared to be going about their own business, or rather, coming home from their place of business, and paying no attention to us whatsoever. They might at least have smiled or nodded.

'We're not at home, honey, we're guests in this country. You've got to be more careful.' Arnold frowned censoriously. 'And I don't think you should have used that language to the bus conductor –'

'Arnold, I don't give a rat's ass what you think!'

At least the passers-by weren't deaf. Heads turned in our direction and turned away again swiftly.

'Shhh, *please*, Nancy.' Arnold had gone a dull crimson.

'A-ahem –' The throat-clearing sound came from our offside. We whirled to discover a tall elegant blonde smiling through a gap in the hedge between the two front doors and trying to look as though she had just appeared there and hadn't heard a word of our previous conversation.

'You must be the Harpers,' she said. 'I'm sorry I wasn't here to meet you, but I wasn't sure when you were arriving and it's half-day closing. I'm Lania – Lania Sandgate.' She stepped through the gap,

22

obviously a well-used short cut, and extended her hand.

'Oh, sure – ' Arnold grabbed for her hand, dropping the key. 'I'm Arnold, this is Nancy – and these are the twins: Donna and Donald.'

'How nice to meet you.' She turned to me as Arnold bent and groped for the key. 'I've been looking forward to having you here. If there's anything you need or want to know, you mustn't hesitate to call on me.'

'How kind of you.' I matched her tooth for tooth, reserving judgement. My first impression was that she was too soignée but, after the twenty-four hours I'd just put in, even Apple Annie would have seemed like a Riviera sophisticate.

'In fact, perhaps you'd like to come over now and have a cup of tea?'

'Not just now,' I said quickly. 'I'm afraid Donna isn't feeling very well.'

'I'm okay, Mom.' Donna suddenly perked up, eyes sparkling, and beamed at our new neighbour.

'Then perhaps you'd like to come to dinner tomorrow?' Lania Sandgate's smile stiffened, her voice lost a shade of its cordiality.

'We'd love to.' I tried to retrieve the situation. 'We'll all be a bit less jet-lagged by tomorrow. The kids don't know how they're feeling right now – '

'Ooooh!' Donald suddenly stepped over to the side of the path and threw up all over a rose bush.

They kept doing that to me! And it still took me by surprise. I never knew where I was with them. I wondered if I'd ever be able to cope satisfactorily with the peculiarities of twinship. It was eerie when one twin produced the symptoms of an illness and the other one produced the effects. My sole consolation was that they weren't single-cell same-sex twins and the problem was bound to improve as they gained adulthood. I wasn't sure that they'd grow out of it – but at least I'd know which one was going to produce the baby.

'I mustn't keep you any longer – ' Lania backed hastily through the gap in the hedge. 'I'll expect you at about seven tomorrow then.'

I put the twins to bed and stayed with them until they went to sleep, still protesting that they weren't tired. It didn't take long.

When I went back downstairs, I found Arnold had already taken over the small study. His portable typewriter was open on the desk, as was a bottle of duty-free bourbon. At least he had provided two glasses.

'Some day, huh, honey?' He poured a drink and handed it to me.

'I don't want to face another like this in a hurry,' I agreed, blanking out the thought that I'd have to for the return trip. That was almost three months away and we'd have a good rest before then.

I leaned back in the easy chair while Arnold roamed around the room peering at the bookshelves. From where I sat, I could see a couple of shelves of novels, which cheered me immensely. I'd been afraid they were all textbooks and technical books.

'Hey – !' Arnold beamed with delight. 'There's a whole shelf of do-it-yourself books here. All English ones I've never seen before. Maybe I'll find some new ideas.'

'Oh, no!' I groaned as he began pulling out books and piling them on the desk. 'You can't fool around with that here, you know. This isn't our house.'

'I know it. I just want to read them – What's this?' He stretched his arm behind the remaining books and retrieved a photograph in a silver frame.

'It must be the Blake family.' I went over to him and we stood looking down at the four smiling faces. I felt a lump in my throat. They all looked so happy and confident, so unsuspecting of the tragedy ahead of them.

'What do you suppose it was doing back there?'

'It must have been on the desk originally,' I guessed. 'After the accident, Rosemary probably couldn't bear to look at it and she must have just put it behind the books to get it out of the way for the time being.'

'Then she either forgot it,' Arnold pieced the rest of the story together, 'or decided it didn't matter if it stayed there a while longer.'

'It's as good a place as any. Put it back. We wouldn't want her to think we'd been snooping.'

'It's too bad.' Arnold sighed, replacing the photograph. 'They were a nice couple. It's a damn shame.'

For once, I was in complete accord with Arnold. They *were* a nice couple and it *was* a damned shame. I only hoped Rosemary would find some peace and maybe a little happiness in our house in Cranberry Lane.

Three

'Oh no you don't!' I caught Arnold by his pyjama shirt-tail as he tried to slide out of bed in the morning.

'Gee, honey, I'm sorry. I didn't mean to disturb you. I thought I'd leave you and the kids to catch up on some sleep and just get an early train to London and have breakfast there.'

'That's what I thought you thought. Nice try, but it isn't going to work. You're not going to leave me and the kids here alone until we've had a chance to look around and get settled. There's still the shopping to do – provided they decide to open any stores today – and I'm not going to lug heavy bundles all by myself.'

'Oh, yeah, I forgot that.' He tugged experimentally at his shirt-tail, but I held fast.

'Just a couple of days,' I coaxed encouragingly, 'and we should be all sorted out.' I hauled myself upright, ignoring a slight tearing sound, and offered a compromise. 'You can have first go at the bathroom.'

We managed toast and two cups of coffee each before the twins came down to join us. They were not to be fobbed off with cereal, so I had to cook some bacon and eggs I had discovered lurking at the back of the refrigerator.

On second thoughts, it smelled so good frying, I

added a few more rashers and eggs for Arnold and myself.

'*Mmrr-hrrm?*' The faint apologetic throat-clearing sound spun me round to glare indignantly at the back door. Surely Lania wouldn't have the nerve to break in on strangers at the breakfast table? But there was no one there.

'*Mrr-hrmm?*' The sound came again, from somewhere down around my ankles, I realized belatedly. I looked down.

An orange marmalade cat with big green eyes stared up at me in uncertain pleading. One front paw was lifted delicately off the floor as though about to wave a disclaimer that he intended to be any trouble.

'Oh, good heavens! We've forgotten Esmond. You poor darling, you must be starving!'

'*Prr-yah,*' he agreed. He moved a tentative step nearer and blinked hopefully. The message was clear: he didn't mean to intrude, but he would appreciate a bit of breakfast. He was the politest cat I'd ever seen.

'Oh, poor Esmond!' Donna pushed back her chair and swooped at him. He retreated behind the stove.

'He's not much like Errol,' Donald said.

'He's shy, and we're strangers. You shouldn't jump at him like that, Donna. You've got to give him time to get acquainted.'

'Errol isn't shy' Donna said. 'Errol isn't afraid of anybody.'

'Errol is different. He grew up with you hooligans. Esmond has obviously been more gently reared. Come on, Esmond,' I put down a saucer of milk by the edge of the stove to encourage him.

After a long moment, a delicate pink nose appeared

and, when we seemed to be paying no attention, Esmond emerged and settled down to his milk. He wrapped his tail neatly around his paws, closed his eyes, and took dainty appreciative licks.

'Is Esmond a *tom* cat?' Donald asked doubtfully.

'Well . . .' I didn't really want to go into that right now. 'More or less.'

'Mostly less.' Arnold snickered coarsely.

'If you've finished your breakfast – ' I gave him a filthy look – 'why don't you get dressed? Let's get our shopping done early. God knows what hour they'll decide to roll up the sidewalks today.'

'Sure, honey, sure.' Arnold heaved himself to his feet and lumbered towards the door. 'And I'll tell you what – ' He paused and looked back at me. 'We'll hire a car this morning, too. Then we'll be mobile again.'

It turned out to be market day in St Anselm. From having no shops open at all, we were suddenly on overkill. Fresh fruit and vegetables were piled high on trestle tables under striped awnings in the central Square. Around the perimeter, other stalls had been set up where they were selling household goods, old books, bits of junk and antiques all mixed together.

'This – ' I breathed a sigh of happiness – 'is more like it!' We plunged into the midst of the fray. We needed everything, so it didn't matter where we stopped.

We had collected about eight small bags before I noticed that most of the other shoppers had brought their own sturdy shopping bags, or else those baskets on wheels. I wasn't keen on them, but I could see that they were a necessary adjunct to life over here. Fortunately, there was a stall selling bags and carts of all descriptions. I bought one, dumped everything into it, and let the twins fight over who was going to wheel it.

'Tomatoes – ' I eyed the varieties offered and found little placards uniformly describing them as either 'Rock Hard' or 'Little Balls of Sugar'. Neither attribute was what I desired in a tomato.

'How about some more bacon, honey?' Arnold broke in on my deliberations. 'And some cheese? They've got both at that stall over there.'

We had used most of the bacon left for us, so I allowed him to steer us over to the stall – where I found more food for thought. Bacon is bacon – or so I had always presumed. But here were neat piles of strange-looking slices of cuts I had never heard of. The piles were labelled with odd names: back, oyster, collar, green, gammon, middle . . . The only one resembling bacon as I had always known it was labelled 'streaky' – and even that was partially unfamiliar, since it was sliced with the rind still on it and complete with gristle. A larger piece – if I'd had to put a name to it, I would have called it an unsmoked flitch of bacon – was disgustingly identified as 'Belly of Pork'.

'Arnold – ' I swallowed and turned to him. 'Arnold, I think culture shock is setting in. Things are different here.'

'They sure are, honey.' With a beatific smile, Arnold began buying cheese like there was no tomorrow.

'I'll have half a pound of Blue Cheshire,' he began, happily reading off the exotic names. 'Also half a pound of Sage Derby . . . and Red Windsor . . . and

29

Stilton . . . and Ilchester . . . and Red Leicester . . . and Wensleydale . . . and – '

'That's an awful lot of cheese,' Donna pointed·out in a worried tone.

'And Double Gloucester . . .' Arnold continued unheedingly. 'And Farmhouse Cheddar . . . and – '

'Like every large rodent,' I told Donna, 'your father could exist indefinitely on cheese alone. Arnold – ' I gave him a sharp poke in the ribs – 'that's enough!'

'And Curd!' Arnold finished triumphantly. '"Little Miss Muffet sat on a tuffet, eating her curds and whey." I've always wondered what that was. We'll have some tonight.'

The stall-holder was whacking off hunks of cheese with alarming rapidity, as though he wished to serve this maniac and get his money before the men in white coats arrived and dropped the butterfly net over him.

'Oh, uhh – ' Arnold came out of his happy trance as the pile of wrapped wedges·mounted on the counter before him. He glanced at me guiltily. 'Er, did you want some bacon, honey?'

'Not right now,' I said sweetly. 'I think we'll live on cheese soufflés for the next few weeks.'

'We can use it all,' Arnold argued unconvincingly. 'Maybe we can give a party.'

'We don't know anyone here to invite to a party,' I reminded him. 'Although I do agree that five pounds of cheese would be plenty for a party – if we were giving one.'

'Is it really – ' Arnold winced – 'five pounds?'

'Three pounds, seventy, actually, Guv,' the stall-holder said briskly. 'If that'll be all, that is.'

'That's all.' Arnold passed over a ten-pound note and waited for change, avoiding my eyes.

'Maybe Esmond likes cheese, too.' Donna tried to cheer me.

'Lovely lot of English cheeses you've got there.' The stall-holder handed over Arnold's change. 'You won't regret it. But – ' he tempted slyly – 'how about some of these French cheeses? This Brie, now, ripe and ready for eating. So's the Camembert, and the Roule, and – '

'No more today, thank you!' I cut him off and grabbed Arnold's arm as he opened his mouth to buy out the rest of the stall. 'Before we do any more bulk buying, we're going to hire a car.'

We found the Rent-Your-Wheels office without any problems, since it was just off the High Street with a big sign over it. The trouble began when we looked at the cars on offer.

'Gee, honey,' Arnold said, 'I'm not sure we can handle any of these. They all have manual shifts – and five shifts, at that.'

'All we've got, squire,' the salesman said. 'You won't find many automatic transmissions around these parts. Everyone reckons they're too dodgy. You'll cotton on to it fast enough. Look, why don't you slip behind the wheel and take it out for a little spin? You can leave your shopping here.'

'I don't know. We don't have much time to fool around – ' Arnold checked his watch and I knew just what he was thinking. 'Maybe we ought to come back another day.'

'You can forget that, Arnold Harper! You're not going up to London this afternoon and leaving me stranded with the kids in a strange town.' He wasn't going up to London tomorrow, either, but I'd let him find that out later.

'Oh, but honey – '

'Furthermore – ' I rammed home the advantage – 'you know perfectly well we're going to dinner at the Sandgates' tonight. No way could you make it to London, get anything done, and get home again in time for that.'

'Okay, okay! We'll take the frigging car!' he snarled, turning on the salesman so violently the poor man cringed. 'What do I have to sign?'

We drove home with the twins joining me in a chorus of: 'Left! Keep left! They drive on the left over here.'

By the time we pulled up in front of the house, we were all frazzled and limp.

'It's not so hard, honey.' Arnold tried to abdicate. 'You'll get used to it in no time.'

'Tomorrow,' I said firmly, 'we'll spend the day driving around and looking at the local tourist attractions. You and I will take turns behind the wheel – and we'll both get used to it.'

'Aw, but – '

'Please, Daddy,' Donna chimed in. 'You never go anywhere with us.'

'What are you talking about?' Arnold was stung. 'I've brought you all over here to England, haven't I?'

'And now you're going to leave us,' Donald said darkly. 'Again.'

'As usual,' I agreed. 'You see, Arnold, even the kids are on to you.'

'This *is* supposed to be a working trip.' Arnold set

his jaw stubbornly. 'There's an awful lot of research to be done. Those archives contain tons of material. I shouldn't waste a minute getting to them.'

'If you give yourself a couple of days to recover from the jet-lag, you'll be fresher when you get to them. Besides,' I reminded him, 'we don't know how late that dinner at the Sandgates' will run. You may be very happy to sleep late in the morning and then have a lazy day.'

'Maybe.' He was grudging, but I could see that I had persuaded him. 'Well, okay. We'll get that over with tonight and see how we feel in the morning.'

Four

Lania opened the door, greeted us with a wide smile and introduced her husband, Richard, who was hovering at her elbow. He was short, dark and just missed being handsome; there was something about his expression that reminded me of Arnold. I was certain that they were going to be good friends – if Arnold could be dragged away from his research long enough to let a friendship develop.

'And *my* children: Angela and Peregrine.' She beckoned them forward to meet Donna and Donald. 'Now you children run upstairs,' she commanded. 'Mrs Thing will give you supper in the nursery before she leaves and you can watch television.' She turned back to Arnold and me with a moue of distaste. 'They're rerunning *The Wooden Horse* – again. But it does keep the children amused.'

We followed her through the hallway and into the drawing-room with a sense of slightly out-of-whack *déjà vu* becuase the layout was a mirror image of our own quarters. Only to be expected, I suppose, in the sort of house they call semidetached, but it was disconcerting.

Especially as there was nothing mirror image about the decor – other-worldly was a more apt description. The colour scheme was silver, black and a pale, shimmering blue. I felt as though I had stepped into an ice cavern. On the far side of the room, a couple who were obviously our fellow guests sat on a huge silver-grey sofa which could have doubled as an iceberg. Their drinks seemed to be floating on air just below their knees until I took a closer look and realized their glasses were resting on an oval sheet of thick blue-green glass set in a narrow black metal framework.

'Come and meet the others.' Lania strode across the room with superb disregard for the fragile, shimmering, blue carpet.

Arnold moved forward gingerly, as though crossing an ice floe. I kept pace with him, looking nervously at the carpet. If only it had been patterned, we could have tried to step on the darker bits just in case we were trailing dirt into the house. One thing was sure: little Angela and Peregine were never allowed into this room or it would not be in such pristine condition. Not unless English kids were a totally different breed of child.

The man rose from the sofa as we reached it; the woman smiled pleasantly. I caught my breath and slid a sideways look of awe at Lania. I had thought Celia was houseproud, but Lania was Olympic class. Of course, it was possible that she did not actually choose her guests to match the decor; it was quite probable that they had been here before and had dressed for the occasion.

'Hazel Davies – ' We greeted her as the introductions were made. She was wearing a slim black sheath which could have been chosen by a *House Beautiful* photographer to set off the room.

'And Piers Alperton – ' So they weren't together. At least, not married-together. He was just as disconcertingly flawless in a pale silver-grey lounge suit. He was also quite devastating with his blond hair, pale blue eyes and thin aristocratic features. Around one wrist he wore a heavy chain which looked like silver but was probably platinum.

'That's a fine old English name – ' Arnold blundered in like a bull in a china shop. 'As in *The Vision of Piers Plowman*, eh?'

'Actually – ' the man did not actually wince, but he gave that effect – 'my family were landowners. We're in the Domesday Book.'

'Oh – ' Deflated, Arnold sank down on the matching sofa opposite them. I sank down beside him, feeling as though I were going down for the third time. Me, in my shrieking scarlet chiffon, looking as out of place as a pool of blood on the carpet.

'Piers was an old colleague of Richard's before he went off on his own,' Lania explained, bringing us drinks. 'He's an interior designer now.'

'Oh.' A light began to glimmer at the end of a long dark mental passageway. I tried not to stare around the room too obviously.

'It's beautiful – ' Hazel Davies had no such inhibitions. 'Really beautiful, Lania.'

'Yes, I'm frightfully pleased,' Lania agreed. She turned to us. 'Piers uses me as a guinea pig for some of his ideas, I'm afraid. Not that I mind – '

Richard, standing behind us, made a small indeterminate sound. It might have been a growl.

'One of my more successful efforts, I must admit.' Piers took a bow.

'I couldn't be more pleased.' Lania looked around the drawing-room complacently. Her gaze wavered as it got to Arnold.

He had decided that it would be a subtle compliment to wear his Black Watch plaid jacket matched with his dark green gabardine trousers. It was obviously a mistake in this room. It could have been worse. If Lania thought that outfit was bad, wait until she saw him in his Bleeding Madras Bermuda shorts.

'Fair do's – ' Piers Alperton had an attack of modesty. 'The lighting is an important part of the effect – and poor old Blake did a magnificent job.'

'Oh, you're so lucky,' Hazel sighed to Lania. 'Here I am, with an absentee husband who seems to be permanently seconded to the Export Drive, and you're surrounded by able-bodied clever men. That is,' she amended, with a guilty glance towards our half of the house, 'you *were* surrounded.'

Suddenly, you could have cut the atmosphere with a knife.

'Mmm, yes.' Lania set her drink down on the glass table with a definite *clink*. 'I think perhaps it's time for us to go through to the dining-room. Mrs Thing must be ready to serve by now.'

'You're not the only one,' I told Hazel as we filed into the dining-room. 'As soon as I let him off the leash, Arnold is going to disappear into the depths of London and all its specialist libraries and I'm going to be on my own, too.'

'Oh, good!' she said, then recovered quickly. 'I don't mean that – I just mean perhaps we can get together once in a while. I'm very much the new girl in town and everyone else has their own schedules and routines. It would be rather comforting to join forces with another newcomer and moan together over a cup of tea once in a while.'

'I know just what you mean,' I agreed. I had already decided that Lania was not going to prove exactly a soulmate. It was comforting to know that a native of the country felt the same way about her. I was afraid it might just be me and my silly ingrained American prejudices. 'We'll get together just as soon as my jet-lag has worn off.'

We were in the dining-room now and Lania was making traffic-directing signals which somehow relegated each of us to the seat she had intended.

I found myself between Richard and Piers. Arnold was between Lania and Hazel. We smiled at each other falsely as we settled into our chairs and Richard poured the wine while Mrs Thing brought in the gazpacho.

I was already beginning to suspect that the English went by the calendar rather than the thermometer and this was another bit of confirmation. Although it was late June, the weather was damp and chill and I personally would have served a hot soup, if not devilled chicken drumsticks, or something – anything – to try to bring the body temperature up to blood heat.

I exchanged a martyred glance with Arnold as we reached for our soup spoons – and stopped dead.

Okay, I know America is unique in that we usually lay out just one knife, one fork, one spoon – and that's it. I've read the etiquette books clueing you in as to how to conduct yourself at the fancy formal occasions. But, Dear Abbey, Amy Vanderbilt and Emily Post –

you've let me down. I've grasped the fact that you should start at the outside and work your way towards your plate when you're confronted by an unfamiliar array of cutlery. Only – there was another set of cutlery at the *top* of my plate. How about that? Where did those implements sort themselves into the routine?

I glanced across at Arnold and found no help there. No doubt about it, we were just a couple of hicks from the sticks. The only thing to do was to fall back on that other dubious instruction and follow the hostess's lead. But Lania was deep in muted conversation with Piers and giving every indication that she might skip the first course entirely. Perhaps she was dieting and didn't care.

I slid a sideways glance at my host, but he was no help, either. He was glaring at his wife and tearing a roll to pieces.

In despair, I turned to see what Hazel was doing. Thank heavens, she was actually paying attention to the food that had been set in front of her. She was attacking the gazpacho with a giant-sized circular implement, sipping delicately from it as it reached her lips. As on a peak in Darien, I realized why all English-based etiquette books exhorted you never to put the soup spoon in your mouth: if you did, odds were that you'd never be able to get it out again.

Frowning towards Arnold, I picked up the same implement – I could not think of it as a spoon – and began wielding it. With an incredulous expression, he followed my example and we struggled through the soup course.

Like a fool, I relaxed when Mrs Thing carried in a

large casserole and set it before Lania. It was hot and still bubbling from the oven. A cloud of fragrant steam wafted upwards as Lania lfted the lid. Mrs Thing had already set bowls of vegetables on the table and now she carefully carried in a stack of plates, using oven mitts, so they were evidently hot.

Lania dished out and passed round the plates, handling them very cautiously. I took mine gingerly, all I needed was to drop it because it burned my fingers and splash that rich brown gravy all over the white lace tablecloth.

I exchanged glances with Arnold, knowing he feared the same, but we managed successfully. It wasn't until we started eating that we realized that the trap was not in the plate but on it.

My first mouthful told me that this was something new in my experience. I wasn't sure I liked it. I chewed thoughtfully and allowed my gaze to wander to Arnold. He was sawing away at a piece of meat, hampered by a bone in an unexpected place. The mistrustful expression was deepening on his face. He glanced up, met my eyes, and crossed his own eyes briefly in a signal he hadn't used since the early days of our courtship.

I nodded agreement and took another cautious mouthful. The meat was rather dry, faintly sweet with a hint of nutmeg – although that could have been the recipe – and completely unidentifiable.

'Say – ' In desperation, Arnold took the bull by the horns. 'This is pretty unusual. What is it?'

'Oh, I'm so glad you like it.' Fortunately, Lania missed the fine distinction between 'pretty unusual' and a genuine compliment. 'I thought I'd serve you a real old English dish. It's jugged hare.'

'Hare – ?' My throat closed up and I fought to keep from gagging. 'You mean rabbit?' With dismay, I heard my own voice rise to a squeak. '*Bunny* rabbit?'

'That's right.' Lania smiled complacently. 'Although hares are rather more on the wild side and – '

I stopped listening. Rabbit was rabbit – and rabbits were pets where we came from. Oh, I knew some hunters caught and ate them – but not in our circles. Why, we'd bought an Easter Bunny for the twins when they were tiny and when it died several years later, we'd given it a full funeral. To eat it was unthinkable. It would have been like eating the cat or the dog.

'Is anything wrong?' Our silence seemed to get through to Lania.

'Oh, er, no. I was just thinking – ' I temporized hastily. 'I'm afraid it might be a bit rich for the kids – '

'Oh, you don't have to worry about that,' she laughed. 'The children are having sausages and mashed potatoes and baked beans. It's all they ever want to eat. Children are so unadventurous, aren't they?'

Lucky kids. And smart. If Lania served many meals like this, no wonder her kids stuck to something safe. I looked at Arnold again. He was judiciously pushing his meat around his plate, but it was no use. If only she had served cabbage – there isn't much room for concealment under a Brussels sprout.

'It's absolutely delicious,' Hazel said warmly. 'You *must* give me the recipe.'

Lania promptly launched into it while I sent Hazel a grateful glance. I wasn't sure whether Hazel really wanted the recipe or whether she was trying to take the heat off us. I was afraid Arnold's face couldn't stand the strain for much longer, but she had successfully distracted Lania's attention and we could relax and exchange another agonized look.

I studied my own plate and experimentally tried to slide a chunk of rabbit beneath a roast potato. The potato perched there for a moment, then rolled off. There was nothing for it, I was going to have to eat more of the ghastly stuff. I sneaked another look at Arnold's face as he stabbed a morsel of meat with his fork and saw that he had reached the same conclusion.

Fortunately, the others – except perhaps Hazel – seemed unaware of our dilemma. Politeness probably entered into it, too, as we all tried not to stare at each other's unaccustomed table manners. I've heard of two-fisted drinking, but the English went in for two-fisted eating. If I lived for a thousand years, I'd never be able to pile all that food on the back of a fork the way they did.

Somehow, we got through the meal and the rest of the evening. Piers went off with Hazel, ostensibly giving her a lift home.

Lania drew me aside just as we were about to make our own escape.

'By the way,' she said, 'if you're writing to Rosemary at any time, it would be as well not to mention anything about Hazel. And, for heaven's sake, never let Rosemary know that you met Hazel in my house.'

'Sure,' I agreed, feeling too green around the gills to be surprised at anything by then. My only interest was in getting out of there before I disgraced myself.

Arnold and I jostled each other through the gap in the hedge and then through the front door, the twins bringing up the rear. My outraged stomach and psyche both began to heave.

'Arnold,' I choked, 'I think I'm going to be sick.'

'You and me both, Babe.' He propelled me up the stairs. 'After you with the bathroom.'

Five

Of course, the twins thought it was hysterically funny. 'Yeeuch!' they said over breakfast next morning. And, 'Another piece of rabbit, Mom?' They reeled around the table, holding their stomachs, making retching noises and doubling up. There is little that cheers pre-teen monsters so much as catching adults in an awkward moment – especially parents.

'All right, that's enough!' Arnold called a halt – or tried to.

'But what about the bones?' Donald persisted. 'Couldn't you tell there was something wrong from the bones? I mean, the whole skeletal structure is different.'

'You must have noticed. Unless – ' Donna giggled – 'you thought it was cat. They say Chinese resta – '

'Stop it! This minute!' I took up the cudgels as Arnold turned pale. 'Remember, if you make us both so sick we can't face food, you'll have to do your own cooking. And you know what that means. Bread and water for a week!'

It was not quite an empty threat. A bout of 'flu had left both Arnold and myself too incapacitated to stagger out into the kitchen for a couple of days last winter and the twins had had to fend for themselves, not very successfully.

'Not another word. Sit down and eat!'

'Okay.' They subsided into chairs and stirred their cornflakes moodily.

'Well, if we can't talk, can we watch television?' Donald plainly rated television a poor second to tormenting his parents.

'Only because it's time for the news.' Arnold tried to pretend that he was interested himself.

'Be very careful,' I warned as they picked up their dishes and filed into the living-room. 'Don't you dare spill anything.'

My appetite whetted by the carefully-selected English programmes shown on WMUR-TV at home, I had been looking forward to an uninterrupted flow of intelligent presentations over here. Unfortunately, this turned out to be the kind of day when I could have used an interpreter. Even subtitles would have helped. It was as surreal as the Monty Python Show and not nearly so funny.

As we tuned in, the newscaster was talking about something called the Green Pound and the Common Market Agriculture Policy. Confusingly, this was followed by an item about supergrass. Just as I was trying to figure out whether this referred to a new Common Market agricultural product or a superior strain of marijuana, it slipped out that they were talking about some crook who'd given evidence against his former cohorts and had to be hidden away. Just the sort of thing happening with plea-bargaining and turning State's Evidence at home. What else is new?

The next item was an interview with someone who had lived to be one hundred but, unfortunately, had such a regional accent that any potentially useful tips were lost between the glottal stops and dropped consonants. This was followed by a report of a political speech in which one politician slandered and insulted an opposing politician in a manner which would have brought him a three-year sentence in an American court of law.

'It's nice to see the old traditions of decent honest debate are being kept up,' I murmured sarcastically to Arnold.

'Just look at him – ' Arnold was shaking his head in disbelief at the commentator. 'Absolutely deadpan. He doesn't see anything wrong in it.'

'I have a feeling he's used to it.' I had already read a wide selection of English newspapers from varying ends of the social scale. Libel, calumny and character assassination seemed to be the order of the day. They probably got away with it because there wasn't room in the courts for them all to keep suing each other constantly.

The weather followed and that wasn't much better. According to the forecaster, we were going to have some sun, some rain, some cloud, some wind, and possibly some gales. He covered every contingency except an eclipse of the moon and the eruption of a new volcano in the middle of Bond Street. We stared at each other glumly as he wound up.

'Did you get that?' Arnold asked uncertainly.

I looked out of the window. 'I think we're safe if we bank on rain.' It was pouring out there.

'I guess so.' He joined me at the window. We watched raindrops bouncing off the shiny pointed leaves of the holly hedge. 'You still want to take the car out for a few practice runs? It's raining pretty hard.'

'Arnold, I'm beginning to get the suspicion that, if we let the rain stop us, we'll never get anything done in this country.'

'You could be right.'

'Arnold, I'm always right.'

'Left . . . left . . . look out – keep left!' Two days later, the kids were still at it. Like a Greek chorus, they burst into a warning chant every time we approached possible catastrophe. It was beginning to get on our nerves.

'Stop! Stop! There's a red light!'

'God damn it!' Arnold exploded. 'I know what a red light means! It's the same in the States. Can't you kids shut up for five minutes?'

'We're only trying to help,' Donna sulked.

'You can help by keeping quiet.' I was firmly on Arnold's side, even though it was true that he had been a bit slow about braking. But the light had changed very suddenly and all the shouting from the back seat was enough to upset anybody's reflexes. Also the manual clutch *was* rather stiff, I'd had a bit of trouble with it myself.

The light changed and we moved forward and turned into the High Street.

'Hey – ' Arnold slowed and pointed to a crowd of people waiting at a bus stop. 'Isn't that Hazel?'

'Yes, it is!' I, too, was swept by the excitement of seeing a familiar face among so many strangers. 'And she's loaded down with shopping.'

'Hazel – ' We pulled up at the kerb. 'Hop in. We'll give you a lift home.'

'Oh, marvellous, but I hate to take you out of your way.'

'We're in no hurry,' I assured her. Donald swung the back door open and she got in gratefully. 'You seem to be loaded down.'

'I am – and I wasn't fancying that hill. It's a long climb from the bus stop.'

'Look – ' I said on impulse. 'Why don't you come back with us and have tea? Then we'll run you home.'

'Oh!' She gasped with shock. 'I'm not sure I ought to. I mean – thank you, I think not. Not today. Please, I must get home. Here comes the bus. I'll just – ' She reached for the door handle.

'Nonsense!' Arnold slid the car into gear and we began moving. 'We said we'd take you home and we will.'

'It was just a thought.' I was obscurely offended. She hadn't seemed the type to get flustered easily and there was certainly no need for her to behave as though we'd begun making obscene suggestions. What was so unthinkable about coming back and having tea with us?

'I'm sorry, Mrs Harper – Nancy – ' she apologized. 'It's just that – I'm expecting a telephone call.' I might have believed it if there hadn't been such a note of bright invention in her voice. 'My children – they're at boarding school – are supposed to ring this afternoon. About their holidays. I must be home to take the call.'

'That's okay,' I said. 'Maybe another day.' See what kind of reaction that brought.

'Oh, yes, of course. Some other day will be fine.'

I didn't believe a word of it. We nodded at each other and smiled falsely.

'And you must come round to *me*.' That sounded more genuine. 'Let's plan something definite soon.'

'Fine,' Arnold said.

Abruptly, Hazel's face changed. We were negotiating a curve on the crest of a hill. She glanced out the window and shuddered.

'Don't worry,' I said. 'Arnold is really a very good driver.'

'It isn't that – ' She broke off, shook her head and made a hopeless gesture indicating that it was something she could never explain. Probably a touch of acrophobia.

'You'll have to direct me from here,' Arnold told her. 'We don't know our way yet.'

'Of course.' She recovered smoothly and began giving directions crisply. We were really quite near and had pulled up in front of her house in next to no time.

'Thank you so much.' She gathered up her multitudinous bags and parcels and got out quickly.

'Think nothing of it,' Arnold said. 'See you soon.'

We were back at our place and putting our shopping away when I discovered the unfamiliar parcel. I didn't remember buying anything of that shape and I unwrapped it curiously, half-suspecting that Arnold was trying to sneak some more cheese into the house.

'Oh, no!' It was a pair of kidney lamb chops, obviously destined to be someone's supper – Hazel's supper. She must have dropped them getting out of the car and the kids had found them on the floor and thought they were ours.

'Don't worry about it.' Arnold took them from me and rewrapped them. 'I'll run over and return them to her. It won't take long.'

As so often before, I had plenty of time to contemplate the difference between Arnold's definition of time and my own. The twins had eaten and were settled in front of the upstairs television and Arnold still hadn't returned.

I was just beginning to lose my temper when the telephone rang. I flew to answer it. 'You'd better have a damned good explanation!' I snapped.

'Hello?' It was a woman's voice. 'Is that you, Nancy? This is Lania. Is anything wrong?'

'Oh, no,' I said. 'I was just expecting Arnold. What is it?'

'I just wanted to remind you,' she said, 'that it's your day for Mrs Thing tomorrow.'

'Mrs Thing? My day?'

'You *do* know, don't you? Didn't Rosemary tell you? I have Mrs Thing for two days a week and some of the other people around have her for one each. Rosemary – you – have her for one. If you want her, that is.'

'Let me get this straight – ' It sounded too good to be true. 'You mean she comes and does all the housework for me?'

'Well, perhaps not all. You have to watch her, you know. They'll all slack off if you give them the chance. And you pay her at the end of each day – ' She named a sum that sounded very reasonable to me. 'In cash, of course – it's all a fiddle with these people. But so long as you make it quite clear what you want done and supervise her, you ought to be all right. If you want her.'

'Oh, I want her!' There was no doubt about that. One day a week sounded like heaven – I wouldn't have to do much work myself at that rate. 'The only thing is, I won't be here tomorrow. We're all going up to London with Arnold and I'm taking the twins to the Tower and Madame Tussaud's and a few other tourist spots while Arnold does his research. Then we'll meet him again at the end of the day, have dinner in London, and come back on the late train.'

'Quite a full day.' Lania sounded amused. 'Would you like to put Mrs Thing off till another day, then?'

'Oh, no, don't put her off! She can come anyway, can't she? She must have a key and know her way around the place. She'll know what needs to be done.'

'Well, if you're willing to trust her . . .'

'Sure, I'll trust her.' I'd rather trust her than stand over her the way Lania seemed to think necessary. I'd be too embarrassed. 'I'll leave the money on the kitchen table and she can do her cleaning and lock up when she leaves.'

'Very well. If that will suit you, I'm sure it will suit her. I'll give her your instructions.'

'Fine.' I felt I could depend on Lania to take a much tougher line with Mrs Thing than I ever could. We chatted a bit more and I was just hanging up when I heard Arnold's key in the lock.

'Oh . . .' I went out into the hall to meet him. 'So you decided to come home? I thought you'd taken up residence over there.'

51

'Sorry I'm late, honey, but I had a hard time getting away. First, she wanted me to have a drink, then she wanted to explain a few things so that we'd understand. I've got the whole story. Poor woman – she's had a rough time over the past few months.'

'What *are* you talking about?' I pulled Arnold into the study and closed the door behind us, in case the kids got bored with watching television and decided to come downstairs. 'What story? Come on – give.'

'You know Celia told us her sister's husband had died in an automobile accident?'

I nodded.

'Well, it turns out that Hazel was – indirectly – the cause of it. At least, she blames herself. What's worse, Rosemary Blake blames her, too. That's why she didn't want to come into this house. She knows Rosemary would hate to have her under this roof and she doesn't think she ought to take advantage of her absence.'

'How can Hazel blame herself for John's accident?' But that explained her strange behaviour on the dangerous curve. It must have been that very curve –

'Because if John hadn't gone over to her house to do her a favour, he wouldn't have met up with the accident. The lights had fused in her dining-room and he went over to fix them for her. He fixed the wiring okay and had a glass of sherry with her. Poor Hazel still feels guilty about that, but it couldn't have been enough to make any difference. He was driving home when he ran into some maniac on the crest of the hill. That is, the maniac ran into him. John went off the road, over the cliff – and that was that. Hazel can't forgive herself – and Rosemary can't forgive her, either. It sounds as though they had half the town lining up to take sides.'

'No wonder Lania didn't want me to tell Rosemary that we'd met Hazel. Especially not that we met her at a dinner party next door!'

'That's why, all right. In fact, I don't think we should admit we've even heard of Hazel if we ever meet Rosemary. Things would be easier that way.'

'I won't even tell Patrick,' I decided. 'That way, it can never slip out. I wouldn't trust Celia not to snitch.'

'And do you know what else I learned – ?' Arnold's voice took on a note of wistful awe. 'John Blake built an entire room on to the back of this house – wiring and all! It's the room they've thrown their things into and locked off. I'd love to take a good look at it. Do you think we could – '

'Never mind that,' I said. It was bad policy at any time to encourage Arnold in his do-it-yourselfing and I certainly wasn't going to have him start any of that over here. 'Come and have supper now.'

Six

We had a great day in London. It wasn't actually raining – no more than a heavy mist. The corner of the morning newspaper which gave temperatures around the world listed Boston at 95°F, so New Hampshire would be just about the same. I hoped poor Rosemary wasn't melting away in the unaccustomed heat. I felt as perky as a daisy in spring in the damp English summer.

We spent the morning in the British Museum; Arnold in the Reading Room, while I went round the exhibits with the kids. We met up again for lunch at a little Italian restaurant nearby.

After that, Arnold put us into a taxi for the Tower of London and returned to the Reading Room with the air of a man who has done his duty by his loved ones. We'd collect him when the Reading Room closed, have supper and catch a late train, after the rush hour was over. That was the plan.

I took one look at the queue for admittance stretching around the Tower walls and we didn't even get out of the taxi. 'Let's try Madame Tussaud's,' I suggested. The kids didn't mind and the driver was quite cheerful and happy about the idea. When I saw the final total we had clocked up on his meter, I could understand why.

There was a queue waiting to get into Madame Tussaud's, too, but it was a more reasonable length. Besides, it was moving. In the time I had paid off the taxi, it had shuffled forward a good two feet.

'Hurry up, Mom!' Donald grabbed the hand I was holding out for the change the driver was laboriously counting into it and pulled me towards the end of the queue. Donna dashed ahead of us and staked our claim.

Just in time. My incipient protest died as I saw several dozen children pushing out of a school bus and charging for the end of the queue. It was worth forfeiting my change to get ahead of that mob.

'Good thinking, kids,' I gasped, crowding in beside Donna. It gave me a real feeling of accomplishment to look back at the teeming hordes shoving in behind us while a couple of hapless teachers shouted instructions at them.

'We're moving already!' Donna nudged me forward. 'We'll be inside in no time. This is a lot better than the old Tower of London.'

'I think so, too.' There were showcases – more like peepshow cases – embedded in the outer wall, giving glimpses of the delights waiting inside. I gazed bemusedly at a hologram of a skull that turned into a fully-fleshed face as you moved along, then realized the twins were too short to extract full value from it and had to lift them up in turn so that they could view it properly.

'Wow!' Donald said. 'This is swell, Mom. Why didn't we come here first? We'd be inside by now.'

'We were blinded by history,' I admitted. 'But so

was everybody else or we'd be inside the Tower. Don't worry, we'll get there another day.'

By that time, we were turning into the entrance and could see the ticket booth ahead. The line moved forward slowly, punctuated by ripples of amusement. I was fumbling in my bag for my wallet and didn't notice the cause. We moved forward again and I was at the ticket window.

'One adult and two children, please,' I said, pushing my money across the counter.

'Not *her*, Mom!' Donald poked me in the ribs, then turned to glare fiercely at the schoolchildren behind us who had erupted into laughter.

'Oh, sorry – ' I apologized automatically before realizing that I had compounded my idiocy by apologizing to a wax model. It was very lifelike.

'Oh, Mom, you're *funny*!' Donna collapsed in giggles against me. I bought our tickets from an unsmiling clerk for whom the joke had obviously worn thin to the point of disintegration and we headed for the Main Hall. I spotted the next decoy first.

'Go and ask the guard what time it is –.' I pushed Donald towards the figure. He was halfway to it when he caught on and dashed back to pummel my side.

'You were going to! You almost did!' Donna danced with glee.

'I'll get *you*!' Donald tried to thump his twin, but she was too quick for him.

I called them to order and we did the Main Hall and the exhibition set pieces, then headed for the Chamber of Horrors. The twins pressed close to me as we descended the stairs, pointing to the fake cobwebs overhead and the grisly heads of the aristocrats who had been guillotined during the French Revolution. I shuddered as I realized that they were Mme Tussaud's original work; the heads of friends, still dripping with blood, brought straight from the guillotine to the young Marie Tussaud who was forced to model them in wax. How had she kept her sanity?

Yet, there was her own figure: Mme Tussaud herself, in serene old age, self-modelled and smiling. Proving that a strong enough personality could live through anything; survive horrors, emigrate and become a great business success in another country. It was surprising that modern feminists had not adopted her as a patron saint of their cause; she had everything. It would be a pity if a husband and a few children disqualified her.

The huge main line station was deserted and curiously eerie as we walked through it. The shops were shut and dark; only a lone vendor with a pile of evening newspapers was in sight. It was past the rush hour and not yet time for the theatre crowd to be heading for the suburbs.

We found our train platform and, so that we wouldn't have to walk so far at the other end, we strolled almost the length of it, passing endless lighted windows illuminating empty carriages. It might have been a ghost train.

We settled ourselves in a compartment; soon a whistle blew, doors slammed and the train moved slowly out of the station. Arnold settled back and began reading the newspaper, the twins dropped into a light doze. I sat at the window looking out at what I could see of the scenery going past. Vignettes of life appeared and disappeared as the lighted windows flashed by.

I felt tired but restless. It would be nice to have stayed longer in London, taken in a show, and been one of the crowd on the last train home. Perhaps I could organize a childminding swap with Lania; I'd take her kids some evenings when she and Richard wanted to go out, and they could take the twins so that Arnold and I could get to a few theatres while we were here.

I looked across to say something of the sort, but it was too late. Arnold had fallen asleep, too. With a sigh, I twitched the newspaper from his hands and folded it. I'd read it later; I was still finding the glimpses of English life in the houses along the track more interesting than newsprint.

We had left the car in the station car park all day. The car park had been full when we left it there this morning, now there were only a few cars remaining. We relinquished our tickets to the ticket collector and headed gratefully for the car, congratulating ourselves on our forethought.

Yawning, Arnold slid behind the steering wheel. The twins both crowded on to the front seat and battled with the seat belt until it fastened around both of them.

'Are you sure you're awake enough to drive?' I hesitated before getting into the back seat.

'I haven't been asleep.' Arnold was immediately on the defensive. 'I was just resting my eyes.'

'Hmmph!' I got in.

'It isn't easy, poring over old books and manuscripts all day, you know. This isn't a pleasure trip for me –

I'm working!' He let in the clutch and the car lurched forward.

'I suppose I'm not?' I couldn't let him get away with that. 'If you think trailing the twins around the tourist traps is fun, why don't you try it? I'll swap my feet for your eyes any day!'

Arnold ground the gears by way of reply and we took a corner much too sharply. I was glad the twins were safely belted down. I was hurled from one side of the back seat to the other as the car plunged down the street like a bucking bronco.

'For God's sake . . . Arnold . . . Ooof! . . . find the . . . right gear!'

'It *is* in the right gear!' Arnold snarled. 'There's something wrong with the car.'

'Daddy's driving with the emergency brake on,' Donald reported in a calm practical tone that was more irritating than shouting would have been.

Arnold snarled again — wordlessly, fortunately — and wrenched at a knob by his knee. There was a scream of anguished metal and the car immediately dropped into a more sedate progess.

'And you weren't sleeping!' I jeered.

Arnold deliberately muttered something too low for me to catch and took another corner on two wheels.

He was driving too fast and veering to the right, but I decided I'd better not say anything more. He could be pushed just so far. It was time to shut up.

We took the final corner and barrelled along the street as though we were going right past the house. Arnold drove towards the kerb but didn't slow at all.

'Stop!' Donna shouted. 'Daddy — we're here. Stop!'

'I can't!' Arnold had gone pale, a fine film of perspiration broke out on his forehead. His knee was jerking frantically as he pumped the brake. 'It won't stop.'

'The clutch – ' I called out. 'You've got to do something to the clutch before you can brake!'

'The emergency brake,' Donald shouted. '*Now* use the emergency brake!' He grabbed for it.

I could see cars hurtling past at the end of the street. The traffic light farther on had obviously just changed. If we couldn't stop, we'd plunge straight out across that stream of moving traffic.

'Hang on!' Arnold shouted. 'I'm going to – ' he turned the steering wheel sharply. We lurched up over the kerb and across the sidewalk. There was a muted impact as we hit the hedge and the car tried to climb it.

We hung there, halfway up the hedge. Arnold switched off the engine. 'Christ!' he muttered. 'Christ, that was a close one!'

'The emergency brake didn't work, Dad,' Donald informed him unnecessarily. 'You must have broken it, driving with it on.'

'Nothing worked!' Arnold mopped his forehead. 'I'm going to go back and give those car-hire people hell. They've got no right letting a car like this go out on the road.'

'Oh-oh!' Donna was looking through the hedge. The porch light had snapped on in the other half of the house. 'I think we're in trouble, Dad.'

We were. Lania stormed down the path and shrieked with dismay as she saw the car hanging from her hedge.

'See if you can get out, honey,' Arnold said. 'Easy now. Then we'll lift the kids down. The back wheels are still on the ground. Don't slam the door behind you – we don't want to rock the boat.'

'Okay.' I opened the door and slid out cautiously, trying to avoid Lania's accusing gaze.

'My hedge!' Lania wailed. 'Look at what you've done to it!'

'We're awfully sorry.' I was too busy getting the kids to safety to bother glancing at the hedge, although I sure could feel it. The sharp holly points scratched at me as I leaned into it to catch first Donna and lower her to the ground, then Donald.

'It took years to grow that hedge. *Years* – and now look at it!'

'I apologize – ' With the children safe, Arnold now opened his own door and scrambled out. 'I apologize deeply, Mrs Sandgate, but there was no alternative.'

'No alternative?' Lania wasn't going to accept a feeble excuse like that. If we'd had any decency, we would have driven past and killed ourselves.

'Arnold isn't used to manual clutch – ' I said.

'The brake wouldn't hold – ' Arnold began.

'*Damn* your clutch! *And* your brake!' Lania's voice rose to a fishwife's shriek. 'What about my hedge?'

The twins had dashed for the neutral zone under the portico and were busy pretending that they had never seen any of us before in their lives.

'We'll get on to a garage right away,' Arnold promised. 'They'll send a tow truck for the car. Once they've lifted it off, we can see what the damage is. It may not be as bad as it looks.'

'It looks better already,' I said brightly. 'Now that we've got our combined weight out of the car.'

'Sure it does, Babe.' Arnold slid his arm around my

61

waist and I clung to him limply, even though he was pretty limp himself. We propped each other up in the face of Lania's awesome wrath. There was something inhuman about it. You'd think she'd be glad the hedge was there – it had quite possibly saved our lives.

'I'm sure the hedge can be fixed,' I offered weakly.

'Sure, it can,' Arnold echoed.

'You know *nothing* about it!' Lania turned on her heel. 'Nothing at all!'

Seven

We spent the next few days lying very low. We all but crawled into a hole and pulled the top over us. I caught Arnold actually tiptoeing down the path on his way to the train one morning, hunched over and trying to lower his profile beneath the top of the ruined hedge.

The car-hire people had not been exactly warm and supportive, either. They claimed that there had been nothing wrong with their car – until we got at it. They were in no hurry to let us have a replacement car and, anyway, we decided it would be better to stick to the car we knew. The garage promised to let us have it back by the end of the week with everything fixed. It would be safer to keep it – who knew what problems we might find with another car?

Arnold had even promised to take a couple of days away from his research and drive us around some more. To that end, we were poring over maps at the breakfast table the day the car was due to be returned.

'They sure have some funny names in this country,' Donald observed. 'Lower Slaughter – isn't that crazy?'

'No crazier than Medicine Hat,' Arnold said. 'Or how about the Susquehanna River?'

'Just the same – ' I was studying the map and weighed in on Donald's side. 'I'm glad we didn't have to tell our friends we were spending the summer at Potter's Bar – or Pratt's Bottom.'

'Yeah,' Arnold retorted swiftly. 'We'd have been the butt of some pretty awful jokes.'

We all groaned and hurled pieces of toast at him – the Harper accolade for a successful pun. (Even our friends in New Hampshire had gotten into the spirit of the thing and, during cocktail hour, joined us in bombarding him with olives, peanuts and lightweight snacks. Hostesses had been known to draw Arnold aside and implore, 'Please, Arnold, no puns unless you're standing on the linoleum.')

Esmond took one horrified look at the flying crusts, abandoned his soggy corn flakes and disappeared through the cat flap.

'Oh, look – ' I protested. 'Now we've frightened Esmond again.'

'Esmond is a scaredy-cat,' Donna said severely.

'He's no fun at all,' Donald complained. 'He's afraid of everything. I don't see why we couldn't have brought good old Errol along with us.'

'I've explained a dozen times – ' I explained again. 'The English are paranoiac about rabies, so they have strict quarantine laws. Errol would have had to go into quarantine for six months – and we aren't even going to be here that long. It's much better for him to stay at home where he's happy and comfortable. Also – ' I cut off the incipient protest – 'the Blakes couldn't take Esmond with them because, although he'd be all right going into America if he had a vet's certificate saying he was in good health, he'd still have to go into quarantine for six months when he came back here. It wouldn't be fair to him – or to them.'

'It's a stupid law,' Donald muttered.

'Maybe, but it's the law,' Arnold said. 'We've got to abide by it.'

'Well,' Donna said, 'if we can't have any fun with Esmond, can we go over and play with Angela and Perry?'

'I think you'd better hold off for a while longer,' I suggested. 'We aren't exactly Mrs Sandgate's favourite people at the moment. Give her a couple more days to cool down.'

'Then can we have a pair of roller skates?' Donald spoke as though they were settling for a poor second, but I recognized that they had been working towards this question all along.

'Okay,' Arnold agreed, before I could reply. 'Fair enough. You kids learn to skate and keep to yourselves for a while longer. When Angela and Perry see how much fun you're having, they'll want to come over here and play with you.'

'Over Lania's dead body,' I muttered, but nobody was paying any attention.

'Today?' Donald pressed home his advantage. 'This morning?'

'Why not?' Arnold was in a good mood. 'We've got to go shopping, anyway.'

On the way, I mailed a letter I had written to Rosemary concerning several things I'd forgotten to mention about domestic arrangements at Cranberry Lane. While writing, I'd taken the opportunity to give our side of the story about the hedge tactfully –

just in case Lania had written to complain about us. I hoped Rosemary wasn't emotionally involved with the hedge as well, but I doubted it. Necessarily, the hedge encircled the property on Rosemary's side, too, but it was obviously Lania's baby. Even so, it was a shame Arnold couldn't have managed to ram the car into our half of the hedge. Lania would have had less right to complain then.

We stopped at the garage and got a firm promise for the return of the car by the end of the week. This would have been more comforting if there hadn't been an earlier, equally firm, promise that we'd get it back today.

By the time we'd bought the roller skates, finished our other shopping, and found a taxi to take us back to the house, we were not in the best of collective moods.

It didn't help that Lania was outside pruning that damned hedge for about the eighteenth time since it happened. If only she'd leave it alone, it might recover more quickly. As it was, she'd clipped away at the accident spot and the surrounding area until she had destroyed the original outlines and lowered it about two feet – all the while blaming us for the damage.

'Good morning, Mrs Sandgate,' Arnold fawned as we went past.

She gave us a curt nod and a withering look.

Properly withered, we slunk into the house and retreated to the kitchen where we could neither see nor be seen. Unfortunately, we could still hear the sharp vicious snap of the pruning shears.

'What can we do?' Arnold asked plaintively. 'Do

you think we ought to send her a dozen roses – two dozen? We've offered to pay, but she says she doesn't want money.'

'No,' I said, 'she wants blood – preferably yours.'

'Is Dad going to bleed all over the hedge?' Donna asked with interest. 'Will that make it grow faster?'

'Sure it will,' Donald said. 'Lots of the most expensive fertilizer is made with blood. They've got a deal going with the slaughterhouses and –'

'That will be enough!' Arnold thundered.

'I guess he isn't.' Donna sounded disappointed.

'The subject is *closed*.' I backed Arnold's authority, although I might just as well have kept my mouth shut. The twins exchanged a grimace and then fell into silent communion. I knew that, at some level beyond the rest of us, they were still carrying on their private joke. Donna giggled abruptly and her twin wriggled his ears – a new trick he had picked up.

'All right.' Arnold felt it, too. He reached into one of the bags and brought out the roller skates. 'You wanted these –' He dropped them on the table top. 'So why don't you try them on and go out and get some practice.'

'*She's* still out there.' Donna cast an uneasy glance towards the front of the house.

'Then go and play in the next street over –' Arnold was not so exasperated as he sounded. At least he had broken up the silent exchange. 'She won't bother you there.'

'It's started raining again,' Donald reported, turning away from the window.

Esmond minced in through the cat flap, shook himself and settled down to removing the raindrops from his back. Outside, the sudden downpour hurled itself against the windows.

'Well, that settles that.' Arnold shrugged resignedly. To look on the bright side, the accusing *snip-snap* of shears had stopped out front.

I began putting the groceries away.

'*Prr-hmm* . . .' Instantly, Esmond was at my feet as I opened the fridge door. One paw raised in that delicate, diffident manner, he looked up at me pleadingly.

'I'm busy,' I told him. 'If you ask Daddy Arnold nicely, perhaps he'll open one of the tins of cat food we bought for you today.'

Esmond swung to face Arnold. They looked at each other without enthusiasm. But there was no one else. The twins had taken their skates and retreated upstairs to their rooms.

'Oh; all right,' Arnold grumbled. He found the can opener and shook it at Esmond. 'I hope you realize that *real* cats go out and catch their own food. Our Errol would have gone out and bagged himself a rabbit if he was hungry – a squirrel, at the very least.'

Esmond twitched whiskers and tail-tip. He did not like being criticized. For a moment, he looked as though he might spurn the food Arnold was dishing into his saucer, but it had a mackerel base and he decided to overlook Arnold's remarks.

The telephone rang in the study and I went to answer it, Arnold close on my heels. 'If it's her lawyer,' he muttered, 'tell him we don't speak English.' Arnold was still expecting legal repercussions at any moment; but I thought Lania would not go to those lengths.

'Hello, Hazel Davies here – '

'Hazel!' I went limp with relief. 'How nice to hear from you. How are you?'

'I'm fine.' She sounded amused. 'But I gather you've been having a bit of a time with Lania. She's been telling me all about it.'

'I'll just bet she has! Would you like to hear our side?'

'I'd be fascinated. In fact, I'm ringing to invite you both – and the children – over to dinner tomorrow night. If you haven't anything else planned, that is. I'm sorry it's such short notice but – '

'We haven't and we'd love to!' Behind me, Arnold was nodding vehemently. 'I'm sorry – what did you say? I can't hear you.' A strange swooshing noise had started somewhere. I strained to hear what Hazel was saying.

'My line's all right. It must be at your end. Shall we – ?' *swoosh*, swoosh '. . . sevenish, then? I'll look forward to it.'

'Fine, so will we.' I hung up, then realized that the swooshing noise was still going on. It hadn't been the telephone after all. I turned to Arnold.

'What are those kids – ?' There was a tremendous crash in the hall outside. We dashed for the door.

'Oh, no! No!' Donald lay, strangely humped, by the front door, surrounded by shards of pottery. Donna, unable to stop herself, rolled forward on a collision course with him, shrieking.

'Hang on, honey!' Arnold dived to intercept her. He caught one arm and whirled her round, but not before there were several nasty crunching sounds from beneath her roller skates. He picked her up and deposited her gently on the lower steps of the stairs.

Meanwhile, I reached Donald and knelt beside him, checking for broken bones. That terrible hump frightened me. I was afraid to move him. If he had broken his back –

'Is he okay?' Arnold knelt beside me. I could see my fear mirrored in his eyes.

'I don't know. I – I think so.' Reassurance came only because Donna was sitting there unstrapping her skates so calmly. If anything serious were wrong with her twin, she would not have been so placid.

'Oh . . . wow!' Donald moaned and began stirring.

'Take it easy, son,' Arnold said. 'Can you sit up?'

'Yeah, I guess so.' Donald took several deep breaths – he had been more winded than anything – and pushed himself to a sitting position. Now we could see what had lain beneath him, giving him that humped appearance.

'No! Oh, no!' The green Victorian jardiniere, spilling its hoard of umbrellas, was decidedly the worse for wear. There was an enormous crack running from top to midpoint and several large spots gleamed obscenely white around the rim where it had chipped.

'It's not too bad.' Arnold tried to cheer me. 'Maybe we can glue back the bits.' He looked around vaguely.

'And maybe we can't.' I remembered the crunching noises as I saw that two of the largest shards had been ground to powder under the wheels of Donna's skates. 'I hope to God that thing didn't have any sentimental value for the Blakes.'

'We'll replace it,' Arnold said. 'Just be thankful it

wasn't Ming Dynasty. Although – ' His face darkened and he turned to the twins accusingly. 'Even that's going to cost something. Victorian stuff comes high these days.'

'*If* we could ever match it.' I looked despairingly at the fallen jardiniere. It was looking rarer and more valuable by the moment. Furthermore, there were telltale streaks now marring the parquet flooring. 'What on earth did you kids think you were doing, anyway?'

'You told us to try out our skates,' Donald mumbled.

'And it's raining outdoors,' Donna whined. Both of them were on the verge of the ultimate weapon: tears.

I hadn't realized Esmond had followed us into the hallway until I heard an unpleasantly familiar little hacking sound. I whirled around just in time to see him sicking up his dinner in the corner.

'Oh, no,' I wailed. 'Not him, too. Why can't we ever get a cat with a strong stomach?'

'That's it!' Arnold roared. 'Upstairs! To bed! All of you!'

Cat and kids scattered, leaving us to survey the damage in what passed for peace.

'I've just written to Rosemary to break it to her about the hedge.' I gathered up a couple of still-intact chips and tried to fit them into place on the rim of the jardiniere. 'And now – this. I'll have to write again. She'll begin to dread my letters.'

'Give it a couple of days, Babe.' Arnold patted me on the shoulder. 'We'll see what we can do with this tonight and things will look better in the morning.'

Eight

Things *were* better in the morning. Arnold had always been good at jigsaw puzzles and I had discovered that my green eyeshadow was almost the same shade as the jardiniere. I rubbed it well into all the chipped places until they lost their glaring whiteness and acquired a slightly mossy aspect. I could never kid anybody that they were supposed to look like that, but at least it gave the impression – that the damage had been done some time ago. We moved the jardiniere to a darker corner and decided that was as much as we could do for the time being.

'If only we were at home,' I said wistfully, 'we could ask Viv and Hank to find a duplicate jardiniere. It wouldn't take *them* long. We don't even know where to begin to look for one here.'

'If we can't find one,' Arnold said, 'we'll just have to give Rosemary about three times what it's worth and let her find another one herself – or buy something else. Maybe we ought to do that, anyway. For all we know, she doesn't like it, anyway. It may be something she got stuck with – a Christmas present, or a bequest from a relative.'

'Maybe she'll be glad we did it.' Donald was even more optimistic than his father. 'Maybe she's hated it for years and always wanted an excuse to get rid of it.'

'I wouldn't bet on that,' I told him. 'Just keep quiet and eat your breakfast.'

'That's right,' Arnold said. 'Hurry up and finish your breakfast and run out and play.'

'It's still raining –'

'You won't melt. English kids have been playing out in the rain for thousands of years and it hasn't done them any harm.'

'Angela and Perry are out in their backyard now.' I looked out of the window at the exquisitely ordered garden aligned with ours. 'Why don't you go over and play with them? Or, better still, invite them over here – they don't seem to have any swings.'

'Are you kidding? Their mother would kill us.'

'Don't get my hopes up,' I snapped.

'Look, kids –' Arnold intervened. 'I'm the one who was driving. Lania will have it in for me – she won't be so mad at you by now. Just you go ahead out there and see if that isn't so.'

After Arnold had left to catch his train, the twins settled down to play on the swings. I gave them some paper towels to mop the seats, vetoing Donna's sugestion of removing a couple of cushions from the sofa to put on the seats. We would not add muddy cushions to the damage already done.

Sure enough, the prospect of cadging rides on the swings brought Angela and Peregrine first to the dividing fence, then over it and into our yard. If Lania disapproved, she evidently was not about to make an issue of it. Maybe, like me, she felt it was hard enough to keep children entertained on a rainy day and anything that kept them out of the house and happily occupied was not to be discouraged. I wondered why they weren't in school. It was probably some local holiday I didn't know about.

I settled down with another cup of coffee and the morning paper to enjoy a few peaceful moments before I started the chores.

There was the perfunctory ring of the doorbell, then the scrape of a key in the lock. Arnold must have missed his train.

Footsteps came along the hallway, too light and quick for Arnold's. I looked up from my newspaper to see a strange female walk into the kitchen and set down a shopping bag. She was obviously quite at home.

'Oh . . .' After a moment, the blankness cleared and my mind began to function again. I recognized her from Lania's dinner party. 'Good morning, Mrs Thing.'

'Good morning . . . Mrs Harper.' She gave me a strange look. I hoped we were going to get on all right.

'Please, call me Nancy.' I stood up quickly and held out my hand. 'I'm awfully pleased to see you again, Mrs Thing. It's very nice of you to come and help us out.'

'Um . . . yes.' She took my hand tentatively and released it immediately. She didn't seem pleased to see me. Maybe she thought we'd always be out of the house when she came to clean. Come to think of it, I'd prefer it that way, too. Then I wouldn't have to feel guilty about sitting around in my bathrobe with the dishes in the sink and the beds unmade.

'Well . . .' I kept smiling but my mind had gone

blank again. What did I do now? Should I suggest she go ahead with her work? Would that sound insulting? Maybe I ought to offer her a cup of coffee? But I had just emptied the pot and would have to make more.

'Well . . .' She glanced around the kitchen and then at me. 'I expect you'll want to go and get dressed.'

'Oh, yes. Yes, I do,' I said, gratefully leaping at the chance to retreat. 'I'll just . . .'

'Don't bother about me.' She interpreted my hesitation correctly. 'I'll just get on with things down here.' She began clearing the table.

I smiled nervously at her and fled.

I stayed out of sight for as long as I could. When sounds of activity below began to die down, I guessed that she must want to come upstairs and clean up here. Meanwhile, I had made the beds and done some preliminary dusting. It didn't look quite the pigsty it usually did when the twins were around.

'Uh . . .' I went to the head of the stairs. 'I suppose you'd like to do up here now, Mrs Thing?'

'In a minute.' She glared up at me. I had miscalculated. She had not finished. Far from it. She was on her hands and knees in the hallway, scrubbing away at the streaks on the parquet flooring.

'Oh, I'm so sorry about that. The twins had new roller skates and they started trying them out inside the house before I could catch them.' I knew without being told that the Blake children would never ever have dreamed of doing anything like skating indoors. I wondered if she had noticed –

'I see you've moved the jardiniere.' She had. She had probably counted every chip.

'We're going to buy a replacement,' I said guiltily, starting down the stairs. 'And we'll hire a sander before we leave and do the hallway properly. Please, Mrs Thing, don't bother about it. We'll fix it.'

'My name is Mrs Dover — ' She lurched to her feet and glared at me, eye-to-eye. 'Dover, as in the port of.'

'Oh, I'm sorry.' I could feel myself going red. 'I thought — I mean, Lania said — '

'Oh, I know where you got it from, don't worry. I know what that one calls me behind my back. It's all part of the airs and graces she gives herself, making out that she's too above people like me to remember our names. She doesn't dare call me that to my face, I promise you.'

'Oh, dear,' I said. 'I'm so sorry, Mrs Th — Mrs Dover. I do apologize most earnestly.' I was growing furious, with myself as well as with Lania. I should have realized that Thing was an unlikely name from the way Lania had rattled it off.

'Don't worry, I know it's not your fault. And I'll tell you something about that "lady". She's not all she pretends to be — not by any means. Lania — hhmmph!' Mrs Dover sniffed. 'Her real name is Lana — so that just shows you, doesn't it?'

'Er, yes. Yes, indeed,' I agreed cravenly, wondering what I was being shown.

'She stuck the "i" in to make it sound lah-di-dah, but she started out as Lana, all right. And I happen to know for a fact that she's got a sister named Marlene and a brother named Orson. I've seen letters from them. So she needn't go around trying to pretend she's so upper crust. Her and her Mrs Things!'

She turned on her heel and marched up the stairs, nodding her head vehemently at every step, still muttering under her breath.

Thoroughly demoralized, I fled to the kitchen, shook the money for her salary out of my purse and left it on the kitchen table, then checked that the kids were still okay out in the yard.

'I've got an errand to do,' I told them. 'You stay here and be good. Tell Mrs Dover her money is on the kitchen table, if she asks. I'll be back later.' Then I left the house.

There was no doubt about it. No way was I ever going to be in the house again on Mrs Dover's cleaning day.

Nonetheless, as the day wore on, I found myself immoderately cheered by the realization that Lania was only, as Beatrice Lillie had so aptly phrased it, 'Every other inch a lady'.

The knowledge stood me in good stead after dinner that evening. Hazel had served a delicious meal and we had adjourned to the living-room for coffee and liqueurs, the twins settled in a corner with a video game belonging to her absent children. Hazel sent an occasional wistful glance towards them and it occurred to me that she must be very lonely, trying to fit into the life of a new community, with her husband always off on business and the children away at school. I was about to remark sympathetically on this situation when the doorbell rang.

'I'll go – ' Hazel said rather apprehensively – and unnecessarily. Certainly no one else was going to answer the door in her house. She sent us an almost pleading glance and hurried out of the room.

We heard the front door opening and then a babble of voices. One voice rose above the others and I froze. I turned to Arnold and saw that he had paled. We exchanged a look of mutual helplessness and despair. We had been set-up.

As Lania and Richard reached the doorway, Lania was laughing at something he had said. She took one look at us and stopped laughing.

'Don't blame us,' I said quickly. 'This wasn't our idea.'

'Actually – ' Hazel edged them further into the room, closed the door and leaned against it, cutting off any escape for Lania. 'It was my idea. Mine – and Richard's. We felt the awkwardness had gone on long enough. It was an accident, for heaven's sake – and you *do* live next door to each other. You can't carry on like this all summer.'

'That's right,' Richard chimed in. 'Time to kiss and make up – ' He caught the look Lania flashed at him and faltered. 'Well, make up, anyway.'

The silence seemed to go on for ever, punctuated by random bleeps from the corner where the twins, happily oblivious, were annihilating astral aliens.

Lania looked as though she wouldn't mind disposing of a couple of troublesome terrestrial aliens herself.

'Come, come – ' Hazel gave a nervous laugh. '*Please* – ' Her voice quivered with genuine emotion.

'I have so few friends in this town. I can't bear it if you're not speaking to each other.'

'Jolly awkward,' Richard agreed. 'The children playing together, getting on so well – and the parents on the outs.'

'*I'm* not on the outs,' I said pointedly. '*I'm* not not speaking to anyone – and neither is Arnold.'

'There now – ' Richard turned to Lania. 'You see? It's all up to you. What do you say?'

We held our breath.

'Oh, all right,' Lania said ungraciously. She forced a smile. 'It *was* an accident, I know. But I put so much time and effort into coaxing that hedge into shape – '

'That's enough now,' Richard said. 'We're going to forget the hedge and start all over again.' He turned to Hazel. 'How about that coffee and liqueur we were invited for?'

'Coming right up.' Hazel moved swiftly towards the kitchen.

'Well . . .' Lania forced another smile and looked around the room. 'Isn't this cosy?' She found a seat in the farthest corner. Diplomatic relations had been resumed, but it was going to take a while before they went beyond the bare courtesies.

'Just the way it should be,' Richard said expansively. He seemed to be secretly relieved; he had not been at all sure which way his cat would jump.

'Here we are.' Hazel wheeled in the hostess trolley with fresh supplies of coffee and exotic bottles – all unopened. I wondered if this was the first time she had entertained in a long while.

Possibly it was the first time she had entertained in

this house. There was a curiously bandbox look about it. All the furniture was new and shining, the rugs seemed not to have been subjected to any wear and tear. The room had not the conscious spotlessness of Lania's drawing-room, it was more like the impersonal background of a hotel. There were no family photographs on the wall or on any of the gleaming surfaces. Only the video games the twins were playing with gave evidence that there were children somewhere in the background.

That wistful expression on her face when she watched the twins had betrayed how much she missed her children.

On the other hand, she might be enjoying the chance to have an uncluttered home for a few weeks. It would get that lived-in look fast enough when she had her husband and kids back. She might then be wistful about the good old days when she had been running a bachelor-girl establishment, with no one to tidy up after.

'I think you'll like this.' Hazel set a liqueur glass beside my demitasse. 'It's framboise – my favourite.'

A swift glance at both fragile objects gave me the sudden dizzying impression that I was a child again partaking of a doll's tea party. I lifted the glass to my lips and my head cleared – this was no child's drink.

'That's what I call raspberry juice with a kick,' Arnold approved. 'Would you mind telling me where we can find a bottle of this for ourselves?'

'There's a little shop in town – ' Lania cut in before Hazel could reply, unable to resist the temptation to give advice. Hazel caught my eye, smiled, and leaned back and left her to it.

The conversation lost its constraint and went smoothly from that point. By leavetaking, most of the cracks in the Harper-Sandgate relationship had been papered over. We were back on an almost friendly footing again.

'You've been great.' Arnold turned impulsively in the doorway and hugged Hazel. 'You must come to us next time.'

'I'd like that,' Hazel responded warmly. Too warmly. They were right underneath the front porch light and I could see her arms tighten around him.

A nasty little suspicion curled through my mind: Hazel was missing more than her children.

I would take this up with Arnold later. I turned away and caught the look that passed between Lania and Richard. They had noticed, too.

'You can stay, if you like,' I told Arnold sweetly.

'Just coming –' Arnold dropped his hostess guiltily.

'Don't hurry on my account. Any time you want him –' I laughed merrily to Hazel – 'I'll swap him for a rusty toasting fork.'

'Don't tempt me,' she laughed back.

Nine

After all that, it was highly ironic to realize that Lania would have begun speaking to us again on Saturday in the normal course of events.

Not that it was normal for the police to bring Arnold home.

He'd been in London all day – as usual. He'd warned me that he might be a bit late as there were a couple of bookshops in Charing Cross Road he wanted to visit. I knew Arnold when he got into a bookshop – he looked on them as libraries with price tags – he was almost impossible to dislodge until the place closed for the night.

So I wasn't surprised at how late he was. Annoyed, but not surprised.

I turned the oven to its lowest setting and worked off my irritation by whipping cream with a manual eggbeater. When the doorbell rang – just like him to forget his key again – I ignored it. I heard the twins' footsteps racing for the door. Then:

'Hey, Mom – ' Donald shouted gleefully. 'Guess what? Dad's under arrest!'

'I am not!' Arnold bellowed.

I dropped the eggbeater on the table and it rolled to the floor, scattering dollops of cream all the way. I was vaguely aware of a delighted Esmond advancing upon this unexpected largesse as I dashed for the front door.

I took one look at Arnold — held upright by a policeman on either side of him — and screamed. I had never done that before. But I had never seen Arnold in such a condition before, either.

He had a black eye, a large bump on his forehead and a graze on his cheek. One arm was bandaged, his shirt bloodstained, his glasses bent askew. He held himself strangely, as though there might be a cracked rib or two.

'It's all right, honey,' Arnold said. 'It just looks a lot worse than it is.'

'Arnold! What happened?'

'I don't know.' He shook himself free of the policemen. 'I was waiting for the train. There'd been a big game somewhere today and Waterloo Station was full of soccer hooligans. But they were at the other end of the station. I thought we were okay down at my end. There were several of us waiting for the platform gate to open.'

'It was a fight!' Donald's eyes gleamed. 'Did you win, Dad? What do the other guys look like?'

'It was no contest,' Arnold snapped. 'The last thing I remember, there was shouting and suddenly all the hooligans charged towards us. We scattered. I felt a thump between my shoulder blades. It spun me round. Fortunately, I flung my arm up —' He paused thoughtfully and went off into one of those analytical asides that are going to drive me crazy someday.

'It was sheer instinct. My hand went automatically to my throat to protect it. It must be one of those gestures arising from race memories: always protect the jugular vein. I'd had no idea I was going to do it. It was – '

'Arnold!'

'Just as well you did, sir,' one of the policemen said. 'From the looks of your arm, he was stabbing for the heart.'

'Yes, well, that was when I fell and they began kicking me.'

'Arnold!'

'It's okay, honey. The doctor patched me up – ' He swayed abruptly and the policemen closed in on both sides again.

'The doctor wanted to keep him in hospital for twenty-four hours,' the other policeman said, 'but he wouldn't have it. Signed himself out. Said he had to get home to you and the kids. Best if you put him to bed now, though.'

'Yes, yes, of course.'

'Didn't you catch the guys?' Donald had inherited his father's carping nature. He glared at the police accusingly. 'Did you let them get away?'

'We weren't there.' The police were stung. 'We answered a call and got there the same time as the ambulance. The gang had disappeared by then.'

'If I'd been there, I'd of got them,' Donald said savagely. 'They can't do that to my Dad!'

'I'd have got them, too,' Donna echoed.

'Please, kids – ' Arnold was swaying again. 'It's all over. Let it go.'

'Did they get your wallet?' Donna was intensely practical.

'No – they just seemed to be after blood.' Arnold gave a shaky laugh. 'They sure spilled enough of it.'

84

'Did you have to have a transfusion?'

'That's enough, you kids,' I said automatically, but I raised my eyebrows at the policemen, waiting for the answer.

'The doctor said it wasn't necessary.' The policeman's tone hovered between reassurance and disapproval. 'But he's to take it very easy for a couple of weeks. Until the stitches come out.'

'Stitches!'

'Lot of damnfool nonsense,' Arnold said. 'I'll be perfectly all right after a good night's rest.' Again he shook off the policemen and started for the stairs. He achieved two steps before he buckled at the knees.

They were there to catch him.

'Oh, thank you,' I said. 'If you could just help me get him upstairs – ?'

'No problem.' They hoisted Arnold between them and lifted him up the stairs.

I followed behind. So did the twins.

'Look, you kids, why don't you go and watch television, or something?'

It was useless. Real life had suddenly become a lot more exciting than television and they were not going to be fobbed off with what had become a pale imitation.

The policemen carried Arnold into the bedroom and helped me to get him into his pyjamas. In fact, they did all the work. I nearly fell apart when they got his shirt off and I saw the extent of his injuries. If those knives had struck just a few inches closer . . . if he hadn't raised his arm . . .

'The doctor said to give him two of these.' One policeman produced a small envelope from his pocket. 'Two now, and two more every four hours – but don't wake him up to give them to him. If he's sleeping, let him sleep through to morning.'

'And that's another thing – ' Arnold rallied briefly, indignantly. 'I'm only wounded – not feeble-minded. I'm perfectly capable of taking charge of my own medication.'

'Of course, you are, dear.' I popped one of the pills into his mouth as he paused for breath and brought a glass of water up to his lips. He swallowed automatically and I repeated the process with the second pill.

'Good old Nancy – ' He grinned feebly. 'Flo Nightingale could have taken lessons from you.'

'And don't you forget it!' I pushed him back against the pillows gently. He struggled briefly, then relaxed.

'It's good to be home – ' He caught my hand. 'I'm glad I made it back to you, Babe.' His eyes closed.

'I'm glad, too.' I fought against tears. Not in front of the policemen and the twins. Later, when I was alone with Arnold, watching him sleeping . . . counting his breaths . . . realizing how close I had come to losing him . . .

'If there's anything else we can do – ?' one of the policemen suggested.

'No. No, thank you so much. It was good of you to bring him home.' I led the way downstairs. 'Is there – Is there anything else we should do? Does Arnold have to appear in court, or anything?'

'Not unless we catch them.' Something in his voice told me how unlikely that was. 'We'll let you know.' He edged towards the door.

'Fine.' I took the hint and opened the door. 'Thank you again.'

'That's all right.' They nodded and disappeared into the night.

I had barely closed the door behind them, leaning against it for a moment to pull myself together, when the doorbell rang sharply, startling me out of what was left of my wits. I peered suspiciously through the glass. It was Lania.

'Is everything all right?' She came into the hallway eagerly. 'I couldn't help noticing that you had the police here. Is there anything I can do?'

'Everything's under control, thank you,' I lied cheerfully. I had never in my life felt that things were more out of control. She looked at me as though she suspected that.

'But what – ?'

'Arnold had a run-in with some soccer hooligans at Waterloo Station. The police got him patched up and brought him home. It's all right now.'

'I don't know what the world is coming to!' She shook her head. 'It's not safe anywhere – for anyone.'

'Terrible,' I agreed. I found that I was beginning to tremble with delayed shock.

'Mrs Sandgate – Mrs Sandgate – ' The twins thundered down the stairs. 'The soccer hooligans almost killed Daddy!'

'So I've been hearing.' Lania gave me a concerned look. 'Are you sure there's nothing I can do?'

'Mom, I'm hungry,' Donald complained. 'When are we going to eat?'

'I don't know,' I said blankly. 'Soon . . .'

'*That's* something I can do!' Lania pounced on the idea triumphantly. 'I can take the twins next door and feed them. Then they can watch television with

Angela and Peregrine while you pull yourself together. It must have been the most desperate shock for you.'

'It was,' I agreed. 'That would be awfully kind of you, Lania. Are you sure you don't mind?'

She didn't, but the twins' appalled looks told me that they did. They were not prepared to trust themselves to Lania's impromptu cooking.

'Look – ' I said. 'I have a casserole all ready. Let me get it out of the oven and you can just feed them that. Have some yourselves. Arnold won't be eating anything tonight and I – I'm not hungry.'

'I *quite* understand,' she cooed, following me into the kitchen.

Esmond gave a guilty start as we appeared and retreated under the farthest chair, leaving behind a shiningly clean eggbeater in the middle of the kitchen floor. Now I felt guilty.

'Really, this isn't necessary – ' Lania studiously avoided noticing the eggbeater. 'I have plenty of food and I'm only too pleased to – '

'Hey, Mom!' Donald was not so inhibited. 'Esmond's done a great job on the eggbeater. You won't have to bother washing it.'

Lania winced.

'We'll wash it anyway,' I said, hoping she'd believe me. '*And* sterilize it.' I picked it up swiftly and tossed it into the sink.

Lania winced again.

Her-name's-really-Lana-and-she's-only-every-other-inch-a-lady. The mantra flashed through my mind and enabled me to get a grip on the situation. I

88

found the oven gloves and began wrestling the casserole on to a platter.

'Daddy has a black eye and six stitches in his arm.' Donna took over the task of entertaining Lania while I worked. 'And three stitches in his back.'

'How terrible!' Lania was suitably impressed. 'What a frightful thing to happen on your holiday. What will you think of us English?'

'It could have happened anywhere,' I said. 'The world seems to be getting more violent every day. If it isn't one thing, it's another. There's a lot of arson around in the States.'

'Ghastly!' Lania shuddered.

'And Dad's all bruises everywhere – ' Donald wanted his share of the reflected limelight – 'where they kicked him. He's going to let us count them tomorrow when he's feeling better.'

'*Please!*' Now, I shuddered.

'Come and tell Angela and Peregrine all about it.' Lania herded the twins ahead of her. 'They'll be enthralled.'

Ten

When Lania returned the casserole on Monday, it was filled with a concoction of her own.

'She doesn't have any Borgia blood in her, does she?' Arnold eyed it doubtfully.

'And there isn't any disposal unit in this sink.' I stared down at the strange-looking mess. Odd smells were rising from it.

'Please, honey,' Arnold begged, 'put the cover back on it. My stomach's still a bit delicate. That stuff is making me feel queasy.'

As I did so, Esmond strolled in through the cat flap. We looked at him and then at each other in bright surmise.

'Hey – ' Arnold said. 'Maybe this is the week we save on cat food. Here, Esmond – Here, boy – Come and see what we've got for you. All for you.' We sure weren't going to touch it.

Esmond edged forward suspiciously.

In deference to Arnold's fragile stomach, I carried the casserole over to the draining board before scooping a couple of generous spoonfuls into Esmond's bowl.

'There, Esmond, all for you,' I said, setting it down on the floor. 'Yum-yum.'

Esmond halted just short of the bowl and stared at

it. He arched his neck, sniffing, then retreated a few steps. He crouched on his haunches thoughtfully for a minute, then circled the bowl and approached it from the other side. It smelled the same over there, too.

Esmond turned and gave me a nasty look. Then he stretched out his paw and made raking motions towards the bowl. It was a cat's deadliest insult: he was trying to bury the offending dish.

'And so say all of us,' Arnold agreed. 'That cat is smarter than he looks. You'll just have to flush the stuff down the toilet, honey.'

'I can't. It's got bones in it. I'll have to wrap it in newspaper and throw it out with the garbage. And just hope Lania never finds out.'

'Do it when the kids aren't around, then. They talk their heads off to Lania's kids.'

'I know.' They were playing next door now and I was delighted to have them there. Lania swore she didn't mind, in fact, she was pleased that they had turned out to be such good companions for Angela and Peregrine. I hoped she continued to think so when the English schools let out for the month of August and she would have the kids there all day instead of just in the afternoon after school.

I had also discovered how Lania kept her drawing-room such a spotless showcase: the children were never allowed in there. The upstairs was theirs – except for the master bedroom; the downstairs was Lania's. It seemed to work very well – for her. If I tried it, it would be like issuing an invitation to anarchy. The twins needed only a hint that any place was a no-go area for them and it was a copper-bottomed, gold-plated certainty that they would charge in and take it over.

'Please, honey, wait until I'm out of the room before you scrape out that casserole. I can't stand it.'

'Sorry.' I replaced the lid hastily. Arnold was looking a bit green around the gills. 'Why don't you go into the living-room and lie down?'

'That's not a bad idea.' He inched himself off his chair, groaning slightly.

'Wait a minute. Let me help you.' I hurried to him. 'Here, lean on me.'

Poor Arnold had slept most of Sunday. This morning he had got out of bed, in a feeble feint towards dressing and catching the London train. I put my foot down instantly and he had acceded so readily I realized he had wanted me to. We got him downstairs, still in his dressing gown, and after that he had seized up. It was agony for him to move and I tried not to show how frightened I was. He should have stayed in hospital where the experts could look after him. If only he hadn't been so stubborn –

'Not so fast, honey. I can't keep up with you.'

'Sorry.' I slowed to the crawl that was the only speed Arnold could move at today. If he wasn't improved in the next couple of days, I'd get the doctor to send him into hospital whether he liked it or not.

'That's better.' He sighed heavily and tugged at me. 'Not the living-room – let's go in here instead.'

I helped him into the study. It was a smaller, warmer room and I knew he liked it better. I settled him on to the sofa and switched on the electric fire since there was dampness in the air and rain threatened at any moment.

'Do you want a blanket?' I hovered uncertainly. 'Or a book?' Although I didn't approve, I'd even let him have one of the do-it-yourself books if he wanted it. 'Would you rather read or rest?'

'Don't fuss, honey.' Arnold shifted uncomfortably, trying to find a position that imposed the minimum of strain on his wounds. 'Maybe a blanket would be nice. Just over my legs. They're sort of aching. It must be all this dampness.'

'I'll get one.' I rushed upstairs to the bedroom. While I was pulling the biggest softest blanket out of the blanket chest, I heard a faint familiar scrabbling sound somewhere behind me.

Mice! Maybe even rats! Wasn't that all I damned well needed right now? And where was Esmond? This was his job. I snatched up the blanket and hurried downstairs with it.

'Wait a minute – ' Arnold protested as I tossed it at him.

'I'll be right back.' I dashed into the kitchen, caught up an amazed and indignant Esmond and carried him upstairs.

'There!' I set him down on the bedroom floor. 'Time to get to work.' To make sure he did, I closed the bedroom door behind me and left him there. Then I went back to Arnold.

'Mice,' I explained briefly. 'In the bedroom wall. I've left Esmond up there to deal with them.'

'Fat lot of good that will do,' Arnold said. 'That cat wouldn't know what to do with a mouse if it walked up to him and spat in his eye. He'd probably apologize to it for being in its way.'

'Don't sell Esmond short.' I was whistling in the dark, not quite convinced myself, but you have to do the best you can with the material to hand. 'He may have a few bits missing, but he's essentially a cat.'

Arnold shrugged, but his eyes were clouded with worry. I knew there was more bothering him than Esmond's shortcomings.

'Okay,' I said. 'What's the matter?'

'This is going to sound silly – '

'Go ahead.' I just stopped myself from saying that it couldn't sound sillier than a lot of things he said.

'I've been thinking it over and – ' Arnold glanced at me, as though trying to judge how I'd react. 'And, well, there was something *funny* about the way those soccer hooligans came at me.'

'Downright hilarious.'

'No, honey, you know what I mean. Funny peculiar. There was a whole crowd of us waiting for that train – and I wasn't on the outside. They had to push past three or four other people to get at me. I mean, why me?'

'I don't know. Did the police have any theories?'

'I didn't mention it. I mean, I've only been thinking about it the past couple of days and realized that's what happened. Do you think I should tell them?'

'They've probably forgotten all about you by this time.' In the intervening two days, there had been a spectacular murder, a political scandal and an international incident. Arnold's problems weren't likely to be looming very large on the official horizon.

'Probably.' Arnold nodded gloomily.

'Look – ' I had developed a theory of my own. 'Were you the only American in that crowd or were there others?'

'I was the only one.'

'There you are!' That fitted in with my theory. 'It was just a touch of that old anti-American spirit coming to the surface. "Yankee go home!" and all that stuff.'

'But how could they know I was American? They were too far away to hear my accent.'

'Arnold, you *look* American. It's written all over you. You might as well go around wearing a star-spangled shirt and whistling *Yankee Doodle Dandy*. You'd even look hopelessly American in a Savile Row suit.'

'You think so?' Arnold looked into space pensively. 'I've got to admit it, honey – ' He paused and took a deep breath for the confession. 'I'd really love to go home wearing a Savile Row suit.'

'If you do,' I warned, 'I'm buying a Jean Muir dress.'

Arnold brightened perceptibly. 'It's a deal, Babe!'

With Arnold hanging around the house all day, the week took on a different shape. Also, we had the car back, which was a great help. I had to do all the driving but Arnold, once he had painfully settled himself into the passenger seat, seemed perfectly happy there. Too happy – he went everywhere with me.

Of course, that immediately doubled the grocery bills. Arnold is unsafe at any speed in a supermarket. Let me turn my back for one second and he loaded the shopping trolley with enough extras to provision an army.

He was as bad as the twins and they all had the same sneaky trick: they buried their stuff under the things I was buying so that I didn't know what they'd done until I'd reached the checkout cashier and it was too late.

'Okay, you guys – ' I whirled on my brood as the cashier's hand unearthed yet another surprise packet. 'Who the hell put in those pickled eggs?' As though I didn't know.

'I thought they might make an interesting cocktail nibble, honey,' Arnold owned up. Behind him, there was a surreptitious giggle and I turned back to the cashier in time to see her tapping the cash register for half a dozen chocolate bars and a big cake.

'Okay,' I said darkly, 'but I'm confiscating those and only handing them out when you deserve them.'

Another little giggle answered this threat. Arnold was smirking suspiciously, too. What else had they done?

I soon found out. I took one look at the next item the cashier tossed on to the counter and almost fainted. The giggles rose to a crescendo. I swallowed hard and lost my temper.

'Don't you *dare* ring that up!' I thundered at the cashier. Her fingers froze over the cash register.

'I suppose you think that's funny!' I rounded on Arnold and the kids.

They did. They thought it was the funniest thing they'd seen since Errol tangled with a skunk at home and we'd had to spend half a day with clothes pegs over our noses bathing the furious cat in tomato juice.

'And you – !' The cashier had begun to snicker, too. 'I think that's revolting! I don't know how you can sell such a thing. It's obscene!'

'It's a very popular item,' the girl sniffed. 'Particularly among our older customers. They like to make their own brawn.'

'All brawn and no brains,' Arnold muttered. He still thought it was hilarious.

I didn't. I'd seen that . . . that . . . *thing* . . . in the meat compartment and shrunk away in unbelieving horror. And one of my loving family had caught the motion and picked up the item and buried it at the bottom of my shopping trolley – doubtless hoping to send me off my trolley, and damn near succeeding.

It was a pig's head. To be precise – and even more disgusting – a pig's head split in two. It was neatly laid out in a large tray; one half was cloven side up, displaying veins, brains, gristle and all manner of horrifying inner workings; the other half was perhaps worse, it was the head in profile, one evil little eye feebly glittering.

I took a few more deep breaths, trying not to retch. I saw with relief, out of the corner of my own eye, the cashier slip the sickening object out of sight beneath the counter.

'Heh-heh – ' Arnold tried, too late, to turn it into a cough.

'I hate you, Arnold Harper!' I stormed. 'Some day I'm going to do myself a favour and divorce you. And, when I do, I'll make damned sure *you* get custody of those rotten little monsters!'

Eleven

'Please forgive me for telephoning so early, but I just
had to know – ?' Hazel's voice throbbed with concern.
'Are you all right? Is everything all right?'

'All right?' I looked at the telephone receiver
blankly. Arnold and I were having a lazy Sunday
morning. I'd made coffee, toast and scrambled eggs
and brought them upstairs on a tray. We were in bed
surrounded by an assortment of Sunday papers, the
twins curled at the foot of the bed with what passed
for the comics in a couple of the papers, and even
Esmond had joined the party and was disposing of his
share of scrambled eggs and coffee cream. Things
couldn't have been more all right.

'Everything's just fine.' I didn't bother to disguise
the puzzlement in my voice. 'Why shouldn't it be?'

'Oh, forgive me. I'd heard – ' She broke off
abruptly.

'Heard what?'

'Oh, I'm sorry. Someone said – Obviously, she'd
got things wrong. Just forget I said anything.'

'Oh no you don't. Come on, Hazel, you might as
well tell me. The more you don't say, the worse I'll
think it was.'

'I suppose so. Oh, dear,' she wailed, 'I should have
known it was just silly gossip.'

'Hazel –'

'Oh, it's nothing, really. I mean, I know that now. It's just that one of my neighbours was standing in the queue behind you at the supermarket yesterday and she heard – She thought you were serious about . . . about a divorce. And she knew that we were friends –'

'Relax,' I said. 'That was yesterday. I kind of lost my temper. I guess I've got a pretty short fuse –'

'Wouldn't have you any other way, Babe.' Arnold patted my thigh. I leaned back against him, rolling the earpiece to one side so that he could hear the other side of the conversation. No one would have been worried about the state of our alliance if they could have seen us now.

'And they were all deliberately plaguing me –' I went on.

'Heh, heh, heh,' Arnold snickered.

'Anyway –' I gave him a moderately heavy thump on one of the few uninjured parts of his anatomy. 'There's no problem. We're not getting a divorce. Forget it.'

'I'm so glad!' Was she? A faint note in her voice didn't ring true. Inevitably, it brought back the memory of her arms around Arnold under the porch light. Had she called to establish her place in the succession if I was abdicating?

'We kid around a lot,' I said firmly, giving Arnold a dirty look. He responded with a look of injured innocence, not knowing the reason for my sudden hostility.

'Of course, that isn't the only reason I called.' Hazel had recovered herself and was proceeding smoothly.

'There's quite a delightful outing coming up this week. It's been on the stocks for some time, but I'm not sure if anyone has thought to tell you about it.'

'No.' I was intrigued. 'Nobody's said anything to me about any outing.'

'I was afraid not. I know Lania has booked for it, but I wasn't sure that she'd thought to tell you.'

'I suppose we can't be surprised that she isn't rushing to let us in on any treats.' Nevertheless, I felt gloomy about it. 'I guess we really – what do you say? – blotted our copybooks with her, all right.'

'Never mind.' Hazel laughed lightly. 'She'll get over it. I'm sure you'll find she grows friendlier as the hedge grows out again.'

'We won't be here that long.'

'At least, she's on speaking terms again.' Hazel seemed determined to be a little ray of sunshine. 'That's something.'

'Sure.' Lania rallied round in an emergency, and undoubtedly she'd let us know if the house was on fire. But she wasn't exactly what I'd hoped for in the way of neighbours when I left home. I was really missing the friends I'd left behind. Even Celia was beginning to seem like a bosom buddy compared to Lania.

'Anyway, about the day trip. We planned it and booked the coach ages ago, but there are still a few places left. If you're interested, we could fit you in easily. I think you'd enjoy it.'

'Enjoy what?' I was still suspicious. Even Hazel's friendliness might have an ulterior motive. The image of those arms around Arnold, having recurred to me, would not fade. It led to a bemused wonder as to just how she had said goodnight to John Blake the night he met his death. Had she given *him* something to think about that night? So much that he was distracted and not paying attention to his driving when that other driver had come at him? Rosemary had blamed Hazel for his death – was she righter than she knew?

'France – ' The magic word drove everything else out of my mind. 'Boulogne. Shopping. We do it four or five times a year. The coach takes us straight to the supermarket and we pick up our duty-frees and shopping and don't have to worry about carrying it. After that, we have lunch and explore the shops in the centre of town, then catch the last ferry home and are delivered straight to our doors. It makes a nice day's outing.'

'Day? You mean you can do it in a day? Go to France?' I was aware that my voice had risen to a squeak. Arnold and the kids looked at me expectantly.

'The bus will leave here at eight in the morning, it's less than an hour's drive to the coast, the crossing is about seventy-five minutes on the ferry. The coach will take us straight to the supermarket, wait until we've done our shopping, then drive us into town and leave us. We'll make our own way to the ferry at the end of the day – the dock is right across from the main shopping area – and the bus will be on board waiting for us. It couldn't be easier.'

'You've just picked up four more passengers.' Arnold was nodding enthusiastic agreement. 'When do we go?'

'Wednesday. It's a market day in Boulogne, so we'll

have a chance to pick up fresh farm produce and all sorts of lovely things.'

'It sounds like heaven!'

'I'm sure you'll enjoy it. And – ' there was a trace of wistfulness in her voice – 'it will give you a chance to meet a lot more of the townspeople. I know it isn't easy, starting out in a strange country.'

Or even a strange town. Hazel had obviously had her own problems. It was nice of her to be willing to help new people.

'It helps so much,' Hazel insisted, 'if you have someone to show you the ropes.'

'I'd like that,' I said. But would I? Was Hazel taking us under her wing – or attaching herself to us? To Arnold?

'Then I'll see you on Wednesday – ' Her tone begged for contradiction. 'Unless we meet before . . .'

'We'll be there Wednesday morning,' I said firmly. 'With bells on. Thank you for telling us about it.'

I was glad I had something to look forward to, because it rained solidly for the next two days. None of your light 'Scotch mist', either. It was a no-nonsense, heavy, don't-step-outside-unless-you're-prepared-to-swim-for-it soaking rain.

The twins, restless and bored, retreated upstairs to sulk, watch television and play together as best they could until school let out and Angela and Peregrine came over to join them, or they went over there.

Arnold took over the study, stretched out on the sofa, barricaded himself behind piles of do-it-yourself books and – making the most of his convalescence –

called for frequent drinks and snacks. He had decided that nothing but old-fashioned New England rum eggnogs with lashings of rum would console him and bring him back to proper health. Except, when he heard the price I'd had to pay for the rum, he nearly had a relapse.

'*How* much?' he bellowed.

'Please, Arnold, control yourself. It's only money —' A dangerous thing to say to a New England Yankee. 'The scotch and gin weren't that much cheaper.'

'It's outrageous! There ought to be a law!'

'There is — and that's why you're paying so much. It's all taxes.'

'What's the matter, Mom?' The twins, always ready to referee a good fight, had come downstairs to join us.

'Nothing,' I said. 'Your father is simply exercising his lungs — since there's nothing else he's capable of exercising at the moment.'

'It's a swindle!' Arnold raged. 'A government-operated swindle!'

'That's right,' I agreed. 'Now you know why everybody pops across the Channel on shopping trips. As we're going to do on Wednesday.'

'Hey —' Arnold brightened — 'so we are. And —' his jaw tightened — 'we're going to bring back every drop we can carry. Have you got that list of allowances?'

'On the desk — under the brass paperweight.'

Arnold was quite sprightly, almost leaping from the sofa to the desk. The prospect of diddling the government was putting new life into him.

'In the old days,' he said, riffling through the

103

leaflet, 'a man would sail his own boat across the Channel, load up with booze and tobacco – '

'You haven't got a boat and you don't know how to sail.'

'Smuggling – that's the only way to beat them!' Arnold's eyes narrowed. He struck a stance and declaimed: *'Four-and-twenty ponies, trotting through the dark –* '

'That reminds me,' I said. 'Brandy is even more expensive than rum – the best brandy.'

'Ah-ha!' Arnold swung his attention to the twins. They cringed under his sudden calculating scrutiny. *'And they fitted up their cohorts with body-belts for gold, hollow-heeled shoes, coats with secret pockets –* '

'I gotta go look for Esmond,' Donald said uncomfortably. 'I haven't seen him all day. Maybe he's in trouble.' He began hobbling off.

Hobbling? 'Wait a minute,' I said. 'Come back here. What's the matter with you?'

'Nothing – honest.' He paused in the doorway, shaking his head. 'I'm okay, Mom.'

'Then why are you limping?'

'Oh, that – ' He looked to his twin for support. 'That's nothing – just a blister. I'm okay, honest.'

'Me, too.' Donna imitated his gait as she crossed to him. For a fleeting moment, I wondered which one really had the blister.

'Come here – both of you.'

'It's okay, Mom, it burst this morning. I've got a plaster on it.' Donald backed away.

'Me, too.'

'Brandy for the parson – ' Arnold roared suddenly.

"baccy for the clerk – ' He made a sweeping gesture with the wrong arm, paled and staggered. 'Oh, my God – I've burst all my stitches!'

'All right, dear, all right.' I rushed to his side. The twins melted into the hallway. 'Here, lean on me. You're overdoing it. You'd better lie quietly again. Are you sure you're going to be okay for such a long trip on Wednesday?'

'Don't you worry about me.' Arnold collapsed on the sofa with evident relief. 'I'll make it, Babe.' His eyes gleamed with fanatical fervour. 'I won't let you down.'

'Okay, okay.' I lowered him against the cushions and slid my supporting arm away. 'Are you *sure* you're all right?'

'I don't know.' He tugged at the adhesive tape. 'I can't look. Just check, will you, Babe?'

'Easy does it – Steady on – ' I wavered between cultures as I inched the tape away from the wound. 'we're doing fine – '

'You mean *I'm* doing fine – ' Arnold opened one indignant eye as I eased the gauze and cotton wool off the stitches. 'Stop sounding like an idiot!'

'Okay, if that's the way you want it.' I ripped the final covering off.

'Aaaagh!'

'You're doing great,' I assured him. 'Not one stitch has burst.'

'Are you sure?' He flexed the muscles of his arm tentatively and winced.

'Positive.' I began replacing the bandages. A flicker of ginger movement by the door caught my eye.

'Esmond!' White whiskers twitched and a furry

head began backing out of sight. 'The twins are looking for you.' Esmond was unconcerned by this information. If anything, it hastened his retreat.

'You just go and catch those mice – ' I called after him. There had been faint off-and-on scrabbling noises all day, now that I came to think of it. 'What do you think you're here for?'

'Call that a cat?' Arnold was restored to good humour. He even sealed down the edges of the adhesive tape himself. 'I'd like to see him tangle with Errol. He'd never know what hit him.'

'That's not fair! Errol is – is – ' Suddenly, homesickness swept over me. I wanted Errol and our house in Cranberry Lane. I wanted Pixie tootling the *Habañera* on the horn of the Welcome Wagon as a signal to come out and go for a ride with her. I wanted to know what was happening to Patrick – and even Celia.

'Excuse me – ' I broke away and ran from the study. 'I have to write some letters.'

Twelve

It was still wet and watery on Wednesday, but I didn't care. I didn't even mind getting breakfast ready an hour and a half ahead of time.

'Are we still going to go?' Donna worried nervously. 'It's raining outside.'

'This is England,' I said. 'If they let a little thing like rain stop them, they'd never get anything done. They'd still be living in the Dark Ages.'

'*Through rain and sleet and gloom of night –* ' Arnold began quoting, neatly mixing an entire nation up with the United States Postal Service.

'That's right, dear.' Under the guise of putting more toast on his plate, I managed to slide my hand across his forehead to try to assess his temperature. It seemed to be within reasonable limits, but I realized I would have to keep a close watch on him. He was not as normal as he was trying to pretend.

'Angela and Peregrine have to go to school today,' Donna informed us complacently. 'They're furious because they can't come.'

'Too bad,' Arnold said mechanically, buttering another slice of toast. Beside him, a pad of paper was covered with oblique calculations about the exchange rate, comparative prices according to the brochure he had picked up in a travel agency, and the current state of the Harper budget. He took a large bite of toast and jotted down a few more figures.

'*We* don't have to go to school in summer,' Donald said smugly. 'Angela and Perry would love to move over to the States to live.'

'Fine.' I poured more milk into his glass. 'Just let them convince their parents to move.' (And *don't* let them move anywhere near New Hampshire. I'd already had enough of dear Lania to last me a lifetime.)

'Oh, hurry – ' Donna was jiggling with impatience. 'We'll miss the bus. They'll go without us.'

'We've got plenty of time, honey.' But Arnold began clearing his place, putting his notes into his pockets. Donald gulped down his milk.

'Not so fast – you'll choke.' The remark could have been addressed to either husband or child. Arnold was now demolishing his toast at a rate of knots. I looked at them both suspiciously.

'Are you sure you're feeling well enough for this trip, Arnold?'

'Sure, honey. There's no problem. Somebody else is doing the driving. I'll be sitting down most of the way, then we'll just have a gentle stroll around Boulogne. If I get tired, we can go into a café and have a drink and a rest.'

'Well . . .' I transferred my concern to Donald. 'Are *you* all right for walking around? How's your blister?'

'Huh?' He looked at me blankly, then recovered. 'Oh, that. I told you. It's okay now. All gone. I'm fine.' He pushed back his chair and darted for the bathroom.

I watched him closely. He didn't seem to be limping this morning. Maybe he was doing okay, or maybe – I looked at Donna. She had no trace of a limp, either. Whatever had been bothering them had obviously cleared up of its own accord.

Nevertheless, I resolved to keep a careful eye on my little flock and make sure they didn't overdo things in the excitement of the outing.

The coach was loading as we got there. I sent Arnold and the kids ahead to get seats while I parked the car. Most of the passengers seemed to know each other and there were cries of greeting, jokes and much happy laughter.

Hazel was standing to one side – with the party but not of it. She acknowledged greetings, but stayed where she was. Until Arnold came along. Then she moved forward and touched his arm. He turned and smiled down at her; the twins welcomed her enthusiastically. She walked to the coach with them and they all boarded together. *She* might have been the woman of that family.

I parked the car in record time and dashed on to the coach. At least she hadn't had the nerve to usurp my seat beside Arnold. Not yet. She was sitting, however, in the seat directly across the aisle. I gave her a frosty smile (I'd picked it up from Lania) and sank into my seat firmly.

'Would you like to change places, honey?' Arnold had bagged the window seat and the offer was half-hearted.

'No, thanks, this is fine.' It cut Arnold off from the chance of chummy conversation with Hazel all the way to the coast. Of course, that meant that I was stuck with passing the occasional comment and I determined that it was going to be *very* occasional.

'Heavens,' I said to Hazel. 'I'm exhausted. It's such a rush getting everyone ready on time . . .' I leaned back against the seat and closed my eyes.

The twins had taken the seat immediately in front of us and were squabbling already. I kept my eyes closed.

'You can take turns – ' Arnold decreed. 'Donna can sit next to the window on the way down and Donald can have it on the way back.'

'It will be dark on the way back,' Donald protested.

'Never mind, there'll be lights along the way and you'll be able to see as much as you want.' They'd probably both fall asleep on the way back, but he wasn't mentioning that. 'That's what your mother and I are going to do.'

Oh no we weren't. Not if Hazel continued to occupy the seat across the aisle. I slitted my eyes and caught her smiling sympathetically at Arnold. Fortunately, he was too busy with the kids to notice.

There was a sudden rustle of suppressed excitement through the coach and I opened my eyes wide, expecting to see that the driver had boarded and we were off.

But it was Lania, looking, as usual, like a fashion plate. Behind her, Piers loomed like a specially-painted backdrop, in faultless casual wear. They both provided complete contrast to the rest of us, who had dressed for comfort and rain. Especially Piers, who might have come from a different planet than the other men in the coach, most of whom were wearing

110

country tweed jackets of a faintly green hue which made them look as though they had moss gently creeping over them.

The only seats remaining were at the back of the coach. Lania and Piers moved down the aisle in stately progression, nodding right and left as they passed their seated friends. Even Arnold and I came in for a gracious nod. I noted a hum of muted comments in their wake, but could not distinguish any words.

'Good news, you lot – ' This time, it *was* the driver. He bounded aboard, beaming. 'Weather's improving down at the coast, the Channel is smooth – and the sun is shining in Boulogne!' He leaped into his seat and started the motor.

There was a spontaneous cheer as the coach rolled off. We were all set for a good day.

I wouldn't have called the Channel smooth myself. In fact, if this was smooth, I'd hate to see rough. The twins were loving every minute of it, however, and Arnold seemed quite happy, so I slumped down on a bench on deck and concentrated on fighting down nausea and trying to be a good sport.

Just as I was losing the battle, Hazel appeared in the distance. She drew a bead on Arnold and went straight to him. Arnold said something to her and she looked over at me, that sympathetic smile coming into play again. Then she laid her hand on Arnold's arm and fluttered her eyelashes up at him. He bent closer to hear what she was saying . . .

It was faster and more effective than Dramamine. I was on my feet before I knew I was thinking about it.

'You're feeling better.' Arnold greeted me as I came up to them. 'I told you it was just a matter of your inner ear adjusting and then you'd be fine.'

'You were *so* right, Arnold,' I cooed, claiming his other arm. 'I don't know *what* I'd do without you.'

Arnold looked considerably startled, but Hazel got the message, all right.

'I was just telling Arnold about an absolutely super little place to eat in Boulogne,' she said hastily.

'Were you?' I smiled at her vaguely. 'How kind of you. But I was thinking it might be fun if we just wandered around by ourselves and made our own discoveries.'

'Oh, yes. Of course.' She seemed to retreat without actually moving. 'That's much the best fun when you're in a new place. I'm sorry I won't be able to show you around. I'd have liked to, but I have an appointment for a fitting with a marvellous little French dressmaker I've discovered. She's making several things for me and it will take a couple of hours.'

'That's *quite* all right – ' I was still cooing and Arnold was beginning to look distinctly nervous. 'We'll manage.'

'Are you sure you're all right, honey?' Arnold asked.

'Positive.' It was true. I felt a lot better. 'Why don't we take a turn around the deck? Where are the kids?'

'They went down to have something to eat. Would you like something?'

'No – ' A sudden lurch of my stomach told me that I mustn't get overconfident. 'I'd rather wait until we land.'

* * *

As we walked into the supermarket, my first reaction was: this is more like it! English supermarkets are all very well, but they lack a lot Americans are used to – like a wide variety of choice, departments other than food, and sheer size. Also, most of them don't have a liquor section.

Arnold came to a rapt halt in front of shelves full of tantalizing bottles, whipped out his pocket calculator and began giving it a workout. It was obvious that he was good for a couple of hours.

'Come on – ' I turned to the kids and found that they had already disappeared. 'Oh, damn!'

'Don't worry, honey, they won't go far.' Arnold picked up a bottle and squinted at the label. 'Try the candy section. I'll wait for you here and you can head them off at the Pass.'

'Good thinking.' I wheeled my cart around and began a systematic quartering of the sales floor until I spotted a familiar form at the end of a row. The lettering on the packet was unfamiliar, but the shape and scent were unmistakable. I wheeled briskly down that aisle, keeping a sharp eye on the turnings.

Sure enough, second turning along, I found them. They had – as I had suspected – taken possession of a trolley of their own and it was already heaped with enough confectionery to keep them in the dentist's chair for the next decade.

'Hey, Mom!' Donald hailed me. 'We're learning French – without even one lesson. *Confiserie* means candy, *chocolat* means chocolate, *gâteau* means cake, *glace* means ice cream – '

'And *Non* means Not Bloody Likely!' I pounced on

113

their trolley and began dealing items back on to the shelves whence they had come.

'Aw, Mom!' Donald made hapless flailing motions as I denuded the trolley. 'We'll pay for it ourselves. You can take it out of our allowance.'

'I'll take it out of your hides if you don't behave yourselves!'

Donna said nothing. Her demeanour suggested that she had not really expected that they could get away with it, but I noticed that her gaze rested longingly on certain things.

'I want to be fair,' I said. 'You can have three things each – but you've got to choose. Your father and I can't afford to buy out the whole store.'

'Okay.' They brightened immediately, but Donald wanted to bargain. 'How about three each – and three together? That would be fair, Mom. Look at all you and Dad are getting.'

'Hmm . . .' I glanced at my empty trolley, knowing that Arnold was already piling his high. 'We'll see . . .' I had better get back and see what Arnold was doing. Not only were his selections going to be a lot more expensive than those of the twins, but they could get us into more serious trouble if we got caught taking them through the Green Lane when we hit English Customs.

Several people hailed me on my way back to Arnold. Hazel had been right: this *was* a good way to get to know more of the townsfolk. There was a common air of camaraderie and shared conspiracy that was already acting as a bonding agent.

'Do you think I could slip this under my belt?' A

woman I had hitherto thought of as a staid member of the community held up a knobbly bottle.

'Go ahead – ' Her friend egged her on. 'I'll say I'm your midwife and Customs will rush us through to get you off the docks before you go into labour and they have to help.'

Both women shrieked with bawdy laughter, clutching at their trolleys for support. A couple who were obviously French regarded them with disdainful amusement.

'Oh, Nancy – ' Lania was lurking around the next turning and decided to condescend. 'Have you seen the Housewares? They're having a sale on Sabatier kitchen knives – they're one of the best value items in any case, so they're twice as good now. I know Rosemary was moaning that her knives weren't as good as they should be – '

'Thanks,' I said. 'I'll check that out.' I refrained from promising that, if I bought any, I'd leave them behind for Rosemary. I could do with some decent kitchen knives in New Hampshire myself. I noticed that Lania's trolley was filled with luxury items and decided to take a quiet leaf from her book: walnut oil, pâtés, cheeses, and some exotic dairy items.

Piers had also gone for the most expensive things on offer. A large tin of truffles nestled beside two bottles of Armagnac, fruits bottled in liqueurs, and the inevitable walnut oil.

'Excuse me,' I said, 'but where did you find the walnut oil?'

They pointed me in the right direction, which was also the gourmet section, and I spent quite a happy half-hour before the thought recurred to me that I had better go and see what Arnold was buying and tell him to stop it. Also to collect some money for all this. There seemed to be no rush – I was still surrounded by people from the coach wherever I went – and I got pleasantly lost trying to find my way back and didn't mind a bit.

Not until I suddenly realized that I had passed the candy section twice and not seen the twins. I kept the uneasiness under control by telling myself that, of course, they'd be with their father by now. I didn't really believe it – and I was right.

Arnold was all by himself with his calculator and his shopping trolley, lost to the world. He looked vaguely amazed at the speed with which I rushed up to him and moved defensively in front of his trolley, lest mine should collide with it.

'Where are the kids?'

'They were here a minute ago.' Arnold looked around absent-mindedly. 'I thought they'd gone back to you.'

'I haven't seen them lately.' Maybe they were hunting for me. It was a favourite trick of theirs. Divide and conquer. Having piled their sweets in Arnold's trolley, they'd get fresh supplies and dump them in mine. With any luck, we'd be through the checkout register before we noticed what they'd done.

Then I remembered that I'd just come past the candy section without seeing them.

'Arnold, they've gone!'

'Gone where?' Arnold was still abstractedly tapping out more calculations. I snatched the calculator out of his hands and got his full, if pained, attention.

'How do I know where? They're not in this supermarket, that's all I know.'

'Take it easy, honey. They must be.' He tried to recapture the calculator, but I shoved it into my shoulder bag and snapped the bag shut.

'Then help me find them. You go along the top of the aisles, I'll go along the bottom. We'll quarter the whole store. You'll see.'

When we came together again, back where we had started from, even Arnold was looking worried. He pulled up his trolley with a clinking of bottles.

'They must have gotten bored and wandered out to the coach,' he said unconvincingly. 'Let's pay for this stuff and get back to the coach. We'll find them there.'

We didn't. The flaw in Arnold's reasoning was clear: if they'd become bored with all the resources of the supermarket spread out before them, they'd have been twice as bored hanging around the coach waiting for everybody to show up.

'Where are they?' I looked around wildly. Everything was strange and unfamiliar. All the signs were in French; all the roads led to unknown destinations. Two small children could so easily slip out of sight and be lost – perhaps for ever.

'Take it easy, honey.' Arnold's voice shook. 'They can't have gone far. We'll find them.'

'Oh, sure. How?'

'Let's ask the driver.' Arnold led the way to the back of the coach where the driver was helping load shopping into the luggage compartment underneath the coach. 'Someone must have seen them.'

'Been too busy, mate.' The driver straightened

with a rueful grin. 'I've had me head buried in there – ' he gestured to the dark recess – 'for the past hour. Haven't seen a thing except carrier bags.'

'Oh, God!' I fought back tears of panic. 'Should we go to the police?'

'It's a little early for that, honey. We haven't even looked properly yet.'

'So how do we look? Where do we look? How can you be so calm? For God's sake, Arnold, they're *your* children!'

By this time, we had collected an interested circle of spectators around us as more and more shoppers returned to the coach with their booty.

'Looking for your nippers?' A latecomer wheeled up an overloaded trolley. 'Twins, aren't they?'

'Yes, yes! Have you seen them?'

'Saw them about three-quarters of an hour ago when I brought my first load out. They were hanging about looking proper cheesed-off. Asked me how much longer before the coach left. Told them it would be about another hour and a half, at least. So they went off and got the local bus back to town.'

'*What?*' I whirled on the hapless man. 'They've gone into Boulogne all by themselves? Why did you let them go?'

'Why not?' He was affronted. 'Nothing to do with me, was it? How was I to know you hadn't said they could?'

'They're just children! Children – ' I turned away. 'This is a foreign country. They don't speak the language. They only have a few francs – '

'They were doing all right.' Someone else spoke, trying to be consoling. 'I saw them buying some

118

sweeties. They gave the cashier some English money and she gave them francs. They had plenty for the bus fare.'

'This is a friendly place,' another woman said. 'Not like some French shopping ports I could name. They'll be all right.'

'The best thing for you to do – ' The driver spoke with weary authority, giving the impression that this was not the first time this had happened to him. 'Take the bus into town yourself and find them. The place isn't all that big. Not if they stick to the centre of town – and they will. If they've changed some money, they probably want to do some shopping on their own. Look for the toy shops and the sweet shops. You can't go wrong.'

'Right – ' Arnold looked uncertainly at our trolley full of carrier bags.

'Just leave that stuff, we'll load it for you. Over there – ' The driver signalled to his French colleague behind the wheel of a local bus. 'The bus is just ready to leave. If you run for it, you'll make it.'

Thirteen

Don't worry, honey, they're sensible kids.' Arnold was still trying to keep up his own spirits as much as mine as we plunged through the streets of Boulogne. 'They can take care of themselves. They know where the ferry is and what time we're scheduled to leave. If we don't find them beforehand, they'll be at the ferry waiting for us when it's time to go.'

'By which time, I'll have had a coronary!' All the stories I had ever read about sinister sailors, tramp steamers, and brutal sea captains who didn't care who was shanghaied to man their vessels, coalesced with memories of a thousand films set in shadowy foreign ports with villains lurking in dark doorways, shady ladies without hearts of gold – or any hearts at all – and unscrupulous lodging-house keepers with direct connections to the white slave traffic. 'My babies!'

'Stop a minute, honey.' Arnold pulled me to a halt. 'Take a deep breath. Maybe you should lean over and put your head between your knees.'

'Oh, thanks very much. People think we're crazy enough now!'

We had been attracting curious stares as we hurtled past strolling pedestrians, wild-eyed and panting, occasionally calling out to unseen children.

'Donald! Donna!' I threw back my head and

screamed out the names for all I was worth. I must have been audible within a quarter-mile radius. A couple of people crossed nervously to the other side of the street.

'Look, honey, I hate to say this – ' Arnold sounded strange. I looked at him sharply and saw that he had gone a peculiar shade of grey. 'But I don't feel very well. Do you think we could sit down for a few minutes? If we sit outside at one of these sidewalk cafés, we'll be able to see the kids if they pass. And maybe, if any of the people from the coach come by, we can get them to help us look.'

'Oh, my God, Arnold, I'm sorry!' He was still convalescent and I had forgotten. 'Your arm! Your back!' I steered him to the nearest table at the edge of the sidewalk. 'Are you going to be all right?'

'Yeah, sure.' Arnold sank gratefully into the chair while I looked around frantically: for the waiter, for the kids, for a policeman, for anyone who could possibly help.

The waiter materialized first and Arnold ordered cognac for both of us. We must have looked as though we needed it; the waiter brought it in record time. Arnold ordered a second round before we touched the first. That came promptly, too.

'Drink up and try to relax, honey.' Arnold set an example, his glass was empty when he set it down and he reached for the next one. 'Try to cheer up. The kids are probably having the time of their lives running around this place. We'll catch up with them back at the ferry.'

'Will we? How do we know they even got the right bus? They can't read French. Maybe they got the wrong bus. They could be in some town fifty miles from here, with no idea of where they are or how to get back. And nobody there will speak English or be able to help them. They'll wander farther and farther away. Alone, frightened, crying – '

I discovered that I was crying myself. Also that my glass had mysteriously emptied.

'Atta, gal,' Arrnold encouraged as I reached for the other glass, sobbing. 'Get it out of your system.'

Except that I seemed to be getting it into my system. The waiter appeared with a fresh brace of cognac and I realized that we had not eaten since breakfast and it was now late afternoon. Very late.

'Arnold – ' I choked. 'Arnold, it will be dark soon. And Donna's only just gotten over being afraid of the dark. She'll – '

'Drink up, Babe.' Arnold patted my hand. 'Then we'll start looking again.'

'We'll never find them. We'll never see them again – never. They're gone for ever. I should never have left them. If they'll only come back, I'll never do it again. I'll take better care of them: I'll – '

'Here they are now,' Arnold said, looking over my shoulder.

'I'll kill them!' I pushed back my chair and whirled to face them. 'Where the hell have you brats been?'

They were eating ice cream – perhaps that was the most infuriating thing about it. They looked at each other and shrugged, then turned winsome smiles on me.

'I was afraid you'd be worried.' Hazel saved us all from infanticide. Until she spoke, I hadn't even noticed she was there. 'We've been looking for you.'

122

'Have you?' I could imagine how much looking the twins had done.

'It was awfully good of you to find the kids and bring them back to us.' Arnold spoke quickly.

'Actually, they found me.' Hazel did not sound exactly pleased about it.

Donna and Donald exchanged their secret twin-smiles again. I found I was clenching my fists. I tried counting silently to ten. It would not do to make a public scene in the middle of Boulogne. The French probably had old-fashioned ideas about murdering children – no matter how richly they deserved it.

'Now see what you've done, you kids,' Arnold scolded mildly. 'You've got your mother all upset. You shouldn't have gone running off on your own like that.'

'We got tired of hanging around,' Donald said.

'Yes, it was very boring.' Donna backed him. 'We didn't want to come all the way to France and then stand around in a boring old supermarket. We wanted to see the country.'

'Oh, you did.' Never mind seeing the country, I was seeing red. 'Well, let me tell you, you're really going to find out the meaning of the word bored. When we get back to England, you're going to be confined to quarters for the next week. And Angela and Peregrine are not going to be allowed to visit you!'

'Aw, Mom –'

'That's enough! You've been thoughtless, disobedient, inconsiderate – and a nuisance to everyone. You can stay up in your rooms and think about how lucky you are that we aren't sending you back to the States so that we can enjoy ourselves in peace for the rest of the summer!'

'Aw, Mom – '

There was just the faintest trace of a satisfied smile on Hazel's face.

Quite frankly, the rest of the week was harder on me than it was on the kids, but I stuck to my guns. The next day we were treated to a double-fit of monumental sulks. By Friday, they had graduated to the sympathy racket.

'It's no use your trying that one again,' I said heartlessly, as they limped wincingly through the kitchen on their way to the back yard for one of the periodic breaths of air they were allowed. 'It isn't going to work.' I had already inspected their feet last night, when they had first begun acting as though they were walking on burning coals.

'If you've blisters, it's your own fault – running all over Boulogne. You're lucky you didn't break a leg – or get hit by a car.'

'The cars drive on the right side of the road over there,' Donald said indignantly. 'It's more dangerous here.'

'Regardless – ' I was not going to be drawn into argument. 'You're lucky you're getting off so lightly. From now on, you'll behave yourselves or take the consequences. If Hazel hadn't found you, you might have gotten hopelessly lost and never found your way back to the ferry.'

'Hazel didn't find us,' Donald corrected, 'we found her.' He sniggered. 'And she didn't like it – '

124

'She was furious.' Donna giggled. 'We spoiled her date with the Invisible Man.'

'And what is that supposed to mean?'

'Nothing.' The twins exchanged glances and went off into such paroxysms of laughter that they had to support each other as they stumbled towards the back door.

Before I could challenge them further, a plaintive howl from Arnold in the study demanded my attention. He sounded as though he was dying in agony but, when I rushed in, he simply required a pot of tea and some toasted buttered scones.

By the end of the weekend, I was a wreck. Those scrabbling, nibbling noises had surfaced again and Esmond steadfastly refused to do his duty. He seemed to think it lese-majesty on my part to suggest that he attend to anything so menial as mousing. I had a couple of long discussions with him, citing our priceless Errol – who would never have been left behind in New Hampshire if it weren't for the callous and cruel English quarantine laws – as a shining example of what a male cat should be. Esmond regarded me coldly throughout these pep talks and disappeared through the cat flap as soon as feline decency permitted.

The situation was not improved when Lania decided to intervene on Sunday evening. Possibly the fact that she had had Angela and Peregrine on her hands all weekend had something to do with her decision. That, and the fact that school holidays were starting.

She sailed into the living-room, Richard in her wake, and began trying to tell me that I was interfer-

ing with the freedom of my children, ruining their
social development and probably marking them for
life.

As I studied her quietly, trying to decide just
where I would like to mark *her* for life, Arnold hastily
moved between us.

'Take it easy, Babe,' he said, out of the corner of
his mouth. 'She means well.'

'I doubt that.' Lania was interested only in her own
comfort, which had been disturbed when part of the
twins' punishment had been the barring of their
friends from the house.

'I can assure you – ' Lania began coldly.

'I have told the twins – ' I was equally cold – 'that
their punishment will last for a week – and it will. I'm
sorry Angela and Peregrine don't like it, but discipline is discipline.'

'I really think you might – '

Esmond saved the situation. He marched triumphantly into the kitchen, a limp object dangling from
his mouth. He came straight up to me and deposited
it at my feet.

'*Rrrr-yah!*' he said proudly.

'Esmond!' I was astonished. 'You've caught the
mouse!'

'Well, well.' Arnold looked down at him with
grudging approval. 'So you're not just a pretty face.'

'Oh, darling Esmond!' I bent and gathered him into
my arms. 'Who's a clever boy, then? Who caught the
nasty mouse that was bothering Mommy?'

'Shrew!' Lania said suddenly.

'*You* should talk!' I snapped back.

'No, no,' Richard said quickly. 'She means it isn't a

mouse – it's a shrew. Or possibly a vole. It isn't a house mouse – it's one of the field mice.'

'I don't care.' I cuddled Esmond defensively. 'At least my lovely Esmond was showing willing.'

'Whatever it was –' Arnold stooped and picked up the thing by the tail. 'I guess we ought to dispose of the corpse. Heh-heh-heh.'

'No, no, darling.' I restrained Esmond as he tried to wriggle free to reclaim his prize. 'You can't eat it – it isn't good for you. I will give my lovely boy a lovely can of sardines. And then he'll go and catch more nasty mice.'

'I hope you have several cartons of sardines,' Lania said coldly. 'The woods are full of shrews.'

I gave her a look that let her know where I thought the biggest shrew of all resided and carried Esmond into the kitchen. I met Arnold at the door on his way back to our guests.

'Just don't use the step-on rubbish bin,' he said. 'I'll empty it first thing in the morning.'

'Thanks.' I carried on into the kitchen and gave Esmond his promised treat. No two ways about it, that cat seemed to have grown in stature and confidence. He knew he'd lived up to expectations and that I was proud of him. His triumphal purr throbbed through the room as he demolished the sardines.

'Plenty more where that came from,' I promised him. 'Just you keep this place mouse-free.'

'*Prrr-yah!*' he agreed.

Fourteen

'White rabbits! White rabbits! White rabbits!' First thing Monday morning, the twins charged into the kitchen, shouting in unison.

'Oh, no! You're not starting that again!' Lania's horrible casserole rose up in my mind again and my stomach prepared to rebel. 'That was weeks ago and I don't want to be reminded of it. The subject is definitely, finally, forevermore closed.'

'Not that, Mom,' Donald said. 'This is different. You're supposed to say, "White rabbits, white rabbits, white rabbits" the first thing on the first day of the month. It brings you lots of good luck – and lots of money.'

'Really? White rabbits, white rabbits, white rabbits!' I'd try anything once.

'No, no, Mom, it's too late. You've already been talking. It has to be the very first thing you say on the first day of the month. Otherwise, it doesn't work. Angie and Perry told us so.'

'Did they?' I should have known there was a catch in it. 'Okay, I'll try again next month.'

'Try what?' Arnold appeared in the doorway, dressed for town, driving everything else out of my mind.

'You're *not* going to try to go up to London today!'

'I've got a lot of work to do, honey, and I've lost a lot of time. I'm feeling much stronger and – ' he forestalled further argument – 'I was okay on the Boulogne trip, so I ought to be okay just going to London. I'll take it very carefully and I'll come back on an early train and not get caught in the rush hour. Don't worry.'

Don't worry. Easy enough to say. I glared at the twins. If it hadn't been for them, we wouldn't have had such a hard time in Boulogne. So hard that it made a trip to London seem easy in comparison.

'Can we go out to play today, Mom?' Donald tried his newly-acquired luck. 'Can we? Please?'

'*May* we?' I corrected automatically.

'May we?' he asked on a note of rising hope. 'Please?'

'No. I said a week and I meant a week. Eat your breakfast and go back upstairs.' I hardened my heart to their pleas, wishing I could forbid Arnold's excursion as easily.

'I'll be all right, honey,' he said reassuringly, catching my thought.

'I'll drive you to the station,' I said grudgingly.

After watching Arnold board the London train safely, I did the shopping. By now, I was able to recognize some faces; more to the point, they recognized me and stopped to chat. Hazel had been right. That day trip to Boulogne had been very useful in getting me integrated with the locals – even if it had nearly torn my nerves to shreds at the time.

I shuddered involuntarily and suddenly wondered what the twins were doing right this minute. I trusted them. Of course, I trusted them to obey the rules. They were being punished and they knew it, and they knew why they were being punished. They wouldn't slip out of the house behind my back, would they?

I decided to skip the bakery – there was a long queue outside – and go straight home. I'd been away for a couple of hours and that was quite long enough. Besides, the postman would have called by now and perhaps there'd be some letters for me. I wasn't exactly homesick now, but I sure missed not knowing what was going on back in New Hampshire.

Mostly, I wanted to know what was happening with Patrick; whether that jealous bitch of a wife of his had managed to pull him back from the edge of a nervous breakdown. Celia had thought she could do it all by herself; she'd fixed it so that I was too far away to be of any help; so what was happening? I hadn't heard a word since I'd left. Was that a silent admission that she had failed?

I ran into Lania in the parking lot; she was parked just a couple of cars away. We observed the amenities and that meant a further delay. Before I broke away, I had promised that Arnold and I would go round on Thursday night for drinks and something she mysteriously referred to as 'the unveiling'.

The twins greeted my return effusively. They had obviously been worrying about their lunch, although they were perfectly capable of making sandwiches for themselves, if necessary.

After I got them fed and out of the way, I decided to make a lemon meringue pie to welcome Arnold home tonight. It was his favourite and he would be exhausted after his first full day back at work. A bit of cosseting wouldn't go amiss.

I was elbow-deep in flour when the doorbell rang. As usual, the twins raced to answer it. I continued rolling out piecrust.

'Hey, Mom – ' Donald shouted suddenly. 'The cops have got Dad again!'

'Oh, no!' He'd overdone it going up on that early train. He'd collapsed! He wasn't as recovered as he thought he was. I covered the distance from the kitchen to the front door in record time and skidded to a stop in front of the familiar tableau.

'Arnold! What's happened?'

'Just a slight accident, madam,' one of the policemen said. They were two different policemen this time. 'He'll be all right.'

'Yeah, honey,' Arnold said absently. 'I'll be all right.'

He looked better than he had the other time. There was no obvious physical damage. True, his trousers were torn, he had a large oil smear on his jacket, and he appeared to have lost his necktie somewhere along the way, but he was basically unmarked.

'What happened?' I demanded again. I was not going to be fobbed off with that famous stiff upper lip. English policemen may be wonderful, but I prefer hard facts to soft words. Especially where my husband is concerned.

'He seems to have slipped and fallen, madam.' The policemen gave up the unequal struggle and let me have it. 'In front of a bus.'

'Arnold!'

'Take it easy, Babe. I'm okay.'

131

'I should never have let you go up to London alone. You're still weak and wobbly. They haven't even taken out the stitches yet. I was insane to let you go!'

'Okay, Babe, okay.' Arnold threw his arm around my shoulders and hugged me tight. I was the only one who could know that he was leaning his full weight on me to hold him up.

'Are they going to throw you into jail, Dad?' Donald was evidently of the opinion that the Strong Arm of the Law was strictly punitive. Where had we gone wrong? When I was a child I was taught that, if I were ever lost, I was to march up to the nearest policeman, recite my name and address – and I would be seen home safely. Up to now, I had always thought I had inculcated this procedure into my children. But they must have been watching too much television. How could a parent teach that the Law was a friendly protective force when, night after night, in every living-room, the police were portrayed as trigger-happy gunslingers intent on vengeance and annihilation?

'No question of that, son.' The policeman spoke between clenched teeth, evidently having had more experience of the problem than I had had. 'Your Dad wasn't feeling well, so we've just brought him home, see?'

'Yes.' Donald backed away uncertainly, the tone rather than the message getting through to him.

'I can't thank you enough – ' Arnold said earnestly. His hand wavered towards his wallet, then dropped as he remembered that you don't tip the police. 'Can we offer you a drink, or something?'

'No, thank you, sir.' Both policemen smiled and

moved towards the door. It would be reward enough for them to get out of here. 'If there's anything else you'd like to add to your statement, you know where to find us.'

'Fine, but I can assure you, the bus driver wasn't at fault in any way.' Arnold shook hands with them. 'Thanks, again. You've been terrific.'

'Our pleasure, sir.' They opened the front door and disappeared.

'Daddy! Daddy!' Donna flung her arms around his waist, leaned her head against it and burst into tears. 'Don't die, Daddy. We need you. We want you to stay with us.'

'Okay, kid, okay.' Arnold patted her shoulder. 'I'm not going to die, I promise you.' There was a new, grim note in his voice. 'You and Donald go upstairs now, you hear? Daddy wants to rest in the study for a while.'

Amazingly, they went. Donald, although not admitting it, obviously as shaken as Donna. I followed Arnold into the study and stood over him as he collapsed into the wing chair.

'Arnold, honey, what is all this? What happened?'

'You're not going to believe this, Babe.'

'Try me.'

'Okay. I didn't fall – I was pushed.'

'Pushed? But how – why? Arnold, be sensible.'

'I am.' He caught my hand and looked at me intently. 'Nancy, we can't kid ourselves any longer. I don't know why, but somebody is deliberately trying to murder me.'

'Don't be silly, Arnold. Nobody here knows you well enough yet to want to murder you. Wait a while.'

'I told you you wouldn't believe me.'

'But, Arnold, it doesn't make sense –'

'Just think about it, Babe. One.' He began ticking the occasions off on his fingers. 'One: a brand new hire-car goes out of control. That could have killed me then and there –' His lips tightened. 'It could have killed all of us.

'Two: I was knifed by those soccer hooligans. I told you, there were lots of other passengers waiting for that train – but they rushed at me deliberately. *I* was the only person they attacked. That might have killed me, if I hadn't been lucky. I'll bear the scars to my dying day – which may not be so far off.'

'Arnold – don't say things like that!' I was getting frightened.

'Three: what happened today.' He dropped his hand and stared into space. 'I was waiting in the queue at the bus stop. I'd worked all morning at the London Library and I was going to get the bus over to the British Museum and have lunch in the Museum Pub before going to the Reading Room. I was standing there, minding my own business, when a bus came along. Not even my bus –'

'Arnold –'

'You can't mistake a good solid push in the back, Babe. It was deliberate. Just as the bus came along –'

'Arnold –'

'But, whoever it was, he outsmarted himself.' Arnold smiled grimly. 'He pushed me between the shoulder blades – hitting me bang on my stitches. That's what saved me. I tell you, Babe, I broke the world record for the standing broad jump there and then. I was obviously intended to fall forward under

134

the wheels. Instead, I leaped a mile and it was the far side of the bus that caught me. I went down, but not under the wheels. It must have been a great disappointment to somebody.'

'But who, Arnold, who? Who on earth could possibly want to kill you?'

'That's what I've been asking myself ever since.' Arnold leaned back and stared at the ceiling, as though the answer might be written up there. 'As you pointed out, nobody here knows me well enough to want to murder me. It can't be anything personal.'

'Yes, dear,' I said soothingly, biding my time to move in and take his temperature. 'And what do the police say about all this?'

'I didn't tell *them*.' Arnold was indignant. 'They'd have thought I was crazy.'

'Well, maybe just a little bit overwrought and exhausted.' I tried to slide my hand across his forehead to see if a fever had developed, but he caught my hand and held it.

'Think about it, Babe,' he urged. 'If it isn't personal, then what is it? I've been thinking ever since it happened.'

'And what have you decided?'

'Think, Babe,' he urged again. 'Doesn't anything strike you as peculiar about this whole setup?'

'What setup?'

'The last man in this house dies,' he said darkly. 'In an automobile accident. That was the first way they tried to get rid of me. Doesn't that make you think?'

'Think what? Arnold, I think you'd better go upstairs and lie down. You'll feel a lot better in the morning.' I kept my voice calm and reasonable; yet, despite myself, cold chills began travelling up and down my spine.

'Something funny's going on.' He struggled to his feet. 'Somebody doesn't want a man in this house. Maybe they don't want anybody here at all – and getting rid of the man is the sure way to get the rest of the family out.'

'But why should anybody want the house empty? I mean, maybe Lania would like to have the whole place to herself – then Piers could have a whole set of showrooms – but she wouldn't, would she? Even if the place were empty, she still couldn't move in and take it over. There are laws. Besides, I don't believe the thought has ever crossed her mind.'

'Maybe not. Maybe the reason is something else entirely, but just think about it. If they'd killed me, you and the kids would have gone straight back to New Hampshire, wouldn't you?'

'Of course,' I admitted. 'We wouldn't want to stay here without you.'

'You see?' He began to sway. I rushed forward to prop him up. He clung to me abstractedly. 'And they killed John Blake so that his family would get out of the house – '.

'They couldn't know that.'

'Couldn't they?' He began to crumple. I braced myself and steered him out into the hallway. I had to get him upstairs to the bedroom while he was still on his feet. I could never manage him if he became a dead weight.

'Okay, okay.' He knew what I was doing and cooperated, as much as he was able, carefully placing

136

one foot in front of the other, matching his steps to mine. He clutched at the stair rail to take some of his weight off me.

'That's fine,' I encouraged. 'We're doing fine.'

'Are we?' At the top of the stairs he stopped and glared at me. 'Your precious Patrick's wife is Rosemary's sister. She arranged this house swap. How do you know it wasn't planned long beforehand? *They'd* know Rosemary would do whatever her sister suggested – once they'd got John out of the way.'

Before I could reply, he gave a sudden sigh and crumpled to the floor at my feet.

Fifteen

The trouble with children – *one* of the troubles with children – is that they're always around. Especially when you don't want them to be. There are times when it's almost impossible to hold a private conversation – and those are just the times when you most desperately want and need to hold such a conversation. Like the next morning.

'Look,' I said, 'why don't you kids run out and play?'

'We don't want to,' Donna said.

'Besides, we're under house arrest,' Donald added.

'Okay, okay, I'll lift the restrictions. You've been punished enough. Now, get out of here.'

'I want to stay with Daddy.' Donna leaned against him lovingly and he winced. As I had already ascertained, there was scarcely an inch of him that wasn't badly bruised and aching.

Nevertheless, I was determined to have a fight with him over what he had insinuated about my Cousin Patrick last night. I had lain awake half the night marshalling my arguments – and I could do without a juvenile audience.

'Why don't you put Dad under house arrest, instead?' Donald asked. 'We're okay – but every time he goes up to London alone something happens.'

'It's not a bad idea,' I said.

'You see?' Arnold muttered. 'Even the kids have noticed it.'

'You must admit, it's been pretty noticeable. We're the only people on this street who have the cops at the door so regularly it's getting monotonous. God knows what the neighbours must think.'

'Perry says – ' Donald began, and broke off as Donna nudged him warningly. Evidently, dear little Peregrine's remarks were something it would be safer not to repeat. Not with me in my present mood. He'd probably picked them up from his mother – and I could just imagine what Lania must be saying.

'Look – ' Arnold pulled out his wallet, resorting to bribery. 'Here's five pounds. Suppose you two go downtown and buy yourselves some ice cream or something.'

'And walk slowly – ' I called out as they snatched the money and raced for the door before Arnold could change his mind.

'Whew!' Arnold closed his eyes as the door slammed shut behind them.

'Now that they've gone, Arnold,' I squared off. 'I'd like you to explain your ridiculous insinuations about Patrick last night.' His eyes were still closed and I looked at him suspiciously. 'Do you remember what you said?'

'I remember,' he said tonelessly. 'I'm sorry about that, honey. I was pretty upset.'

'So am I. How could you have imagined – even if you were delirious – that Patrick could have had anything to do with John Blake's death? And if he'd wanted the house empty, why would Celia have arranged this house swap? Why should anybody want to kill you so that the rest of us would go back to New Hampshire? It would have been easier never to have arranged for us to come over here in the first place. It was a crazy idea, Arnold, absolutely crazy.'

'Okay, I admit it,' he sighed. 'It was crazy – and I was delirious.'

'You sure were! In fact, I'm not sure about you now. You've got a funny look in your eye.'

'Okay, I was out of line taking a cheap shot at Patrick. But, you know, the way you two close together and shut everybody else out *gets* me. It's like the twins, sometimes.'

'Patrick and me?'

'Yes, Patrick and you. You think other people don't notice it? Sometimes, Celia and I feel as though we ought to just go away and drop dead and leave you two to get on with it.'

'Now, wait just a minute! There's never been anything like that between Patrick and me. We're too close. We're more like brother and sister instead of cousins.'

'You see? That's just what I mean. Like the twins. With a private world you're not going to let anyone else into – whether you've married them or not.'

'You're jealous! I always knew Celia was, but I never realized you felt like that.'

'Why not? Because I'm Good Old Arnold, your schmuck of a husband?'

'Arnold!'

'Good Old Arnold – ' he ranted. 'Lost in the nineteenth century – and the best place for him! Do

140

you think I don't know what you say about me? You and Patrick, sniggering together – '

That was when I threw the sugar bowl at him.

He dodged, like the sneak he is, and it shattered against the wall behind him. That was when I remembered that it wasn't mine to throw.

'Now look what you've made me do!'

Esmond had been sitting nervously in a corner, twitching his ears as our voices rose. Now thoroughly demoralized, he dashed through the cat flap and disappeared. I hoped he was going to come back again. It was bad enough to break the sugar bowl – which was probably part of a discontinued line and irreplaceable, but Esmond would be even more irreplaceable.

Arnold pushed back his chair and loomed over me. For a split second, I thought he might be going to hit me, but he just stood there shaking his head.

'It's no good, Babe,' he said. 'We've blown up a first-class fight about something totally irrelevant – although it's probably just as well to clear the air about it. But we're doing it because we can't bear to face the real problem. I've nearly been killed three times now. I've stopped believing in accidents. I'm not *that* accident-prone. It has to have been deliberate. Why? And who?'

'I don't know,' I whispered. 'Oh, Arnold, I can't believe it. And – and I'm frightened.'

'So am I, Babe.' He put his arms around me and rested his head on my shoulder.

'Arnold, it can't be true!'

'You'd rather believe they were all accidents?'

'That doesn't make sense, either. Oh, Arnold, what can we do?'

'I wish to hell I knew.' He released me and stepped back.

'The police – ?'

'You think they'd believe me? They've already got me figured for a nut. The original absent-minded professor, who doesn't look where he's going and always gets into some kind of trouble. Even if I'd died, it would have been no more than they expected.'

'But, Arnold, it's so completely senseless. Who would want to kill you? Did you see anybody, notice anything, when you had those . . . accidents?' I couldn't quite bring myself to say 'murder attempts' – and yet, belief was forcing itself on me. Even Arnold wasn't that clumsy.

'Who was there to see? That's what I keep asking myself. That first time – somebody must have tampered with the brakes while the car was parked in the station parking lot. It was there all day. Anybody could have done it.'

'Somebody might have noticed something. There were the porters, the stationmaster, the girls working in the news-stand –'

'Too late to go asking questions about it now. Who'd remember at this late date? Anyway, the second time, when the soccer hooligans attacked me, there were plenty of witnesses – for all the good they were.'

'Those soccer hooligans!' I shuddered. 'I suppose there weren't any of them around when you got pushed?'

'Believe me, I'd have noticed. I've been keeping a sharp eye out for anyone like that — I'm not getting into *their* way again. No, I was standing in a queue full of nice sober respectable citizens — I thought. Then, one of those pillars of society deliberately tried to push me under that bus.'

'All those attempts were made at railroad stations,' I said thoughtfully. 'Do you think that might have had something to do with it?'

'Not really. A railroad station is just an ideal place for that sort of thing, if you analyse it. Lots of people coming and going, worrying about catching their trains or getting to the office on time, paying no attention to anything going on around them. If they see anything wrong, they won't want to get involved, for fear of being delayed and missing their connections. Anyway, the bus queue was nowhere near a station. I was on my way from the London Library to the British Museum. I was right in the middle of the city.'

'But the same principle holds true,' I said. 'They were all travellers, waiting for their buses, not wanting to get involved and delayed. If they noticed anything at all, if they weren't too preoccupied with their own concerns — '

'*They are crammed and jammed in buses,*' Arnold quoted suddenly. '*And they're each of them alone —* Besides, there wasn't much to see. A quick hard push isn't very noticeable when people are standing close together.'

In the land where the dead dreams go . . . Dead dreams . . . dead husband. It had been so close for Arnold and me; it had been a grim reality for Rose-

143

mary Blake. Maybe this was an unlucky house. Maybe some evil cloud hovered over it and menaced the people beneath its roof, wherever they went.

That was stupid. I pulled myself together. Besides, we were only in one half of the house. The roof stretched over Lania and Richard, too, and they were perfectly all right.

'John Blake died in a car crash.' Arnold returned to the point he had made last night just before he passed out. 'It was a pretty certain bet that, at some time after the funeral, the family would go away for a couple of weeks at least. People usually do. What couldn't be foreseen was us. Celia was the unknown quantity in the equation, arranging a house swap for her sister, so that the Blake house wouldn't stand empty at all. We moved in almost as soon as she left – giving somebody no time to carry out a thorough search of it.'

'Searching for what?'

'How do I know? Blake was some kind of lawyer, wasn't he? Maybe he was keeping evidence about a case here.'

'What evidence? What case?'

'God knows. But there are all sorts of cases reported in the media here every day. Look at all those supercrooks and supergrasses they're always on about. There are millions of pounds missing sometimes. And how about all the spies around? Every time somebody in MI5 sneezes, it turns out he's been working for Russia and sneezing in code for years. Maybe Blake was involved in one of those cases. He could have papers, or tapes –'

'Or microdots! Arnold, we've been living in this

house for weeks. If there was anything obvious, we'd have stumbled over it ages ago. And, if it isn't obvious, how would we know it's what anybody would want?'

'Stop and think a minute, Babe.' Arnold was getting portentous. 'We haven't been living *all* over the house. There's one room we've never looked inside. Who knows what might be in there?'

'The storeroom? Where Rosemary left all their private effects? Oh, now look, Arnold, there wouldn't be anything there. We did that ourselves at home – it's standard operating procedure. I wouldn't like to think that Rosemary was going to walk into our storeroom on some trumped-up excuse and through our personal belongings.'

'There's something else about that room,' Arnold said. 'It's the one Blake built on to the house – all by himself.'

'And you've just been aching for a reason to get in there and have a good nose-around. I might have known it!'

'Where's the key?'

'You've just been dying to get in there – '

'On the contrary, Babe,' he said quietly. 'I'm trying to keep from dying.'

I was right behind him as he swung open the door and stepped into the room. It was lined with built-in bookcases. That was the outstanding feature of the house: bookcases everywhere. From the shelves in the kitchen holding Rosemary's collection of cook-books, to the small freestanding bookcase against the wall of our bedroom containing light literature.

But these bookshelves were only half full. I felt a lump forming in my throat. This room had been built by a man with an eye to the future, a library to be an adjunct to his study, to expand into and fill with books as his life expanded and his library kept pace with his interests. He had never suspected that he had no future.

The next thing I noticed was that the shelves that didn't contain books displayed porcelain. Thank heavens Rosemary hadn't left those fragile breakables outside where the twins could get at them. On second thoughts they probably resided in here permanently, safe from her own children as well. It was a room for the whole family to grow into, in time – time that had been snatched away from them.

It wasn't going to be snatched away from us! I felt a sense of cold purpose. Forewarned was forearmed – and we were now warned, as the Blake family had never been.

'Okay, Arnold,' I said briskly. 'What are we looking for?'

'Something out of place?' Arnold hazarded, stirring a heap of potpourri in a silver rose bowl. A scent of faded roses curled through the room.

There was a pile of suitcases and boxes in one corner, probably containing clothing and personal items. We had done that, too. If Arnold's theory was correct, there was no point in looking into those, because they had been packed and put away after John Blake's death. What we were looking for was something that had been placed – perhaps hidden – in the room while he was still alive.

But what? How can you look around someone

146

else's house and decide what should or shouldn't be there? Especially when you have never met the people.

'Arnold,' I said, 'maybe we're going about this in the wrong way.'

'Okay, so what's the right way?' Arnold tapped the frame of an oil painting hanging in the narrow space between two windows. He lifted it off the hook and turned it over: there was no back covering, no place where anything could be concealed, just bare canvas. He sighed and replaced it.

'We should be thinking about the people concerned, asking questions . . . Arnold, are you listening?'

'Yeah, sure, honey.' He was stroking the windowsill lovingly and I knew I had lost him. 'Just look at the way this joint is dovetailed –'

'Arnold!'

'Asking questions,' he echoed guiltily. 'Yeah, you may be right.' He looked around in defeat. 'I sure can't see anything here that might explain the problem. But who should we ask – and how? We can't go up to people and say, "By the way, you don't happen to know of any reason why John Blake should have been murdered, do you?" It was written off as an accident.'

'No, but maybe we can sort of lead up to it. Start them talking about him and reminiscing. Do you realize, people have barely mentioned him to us?'

'That's hardly surprising. We never knew him. They probably thought it would be tactless, since we're occupying the house for the summer.'

'We'll start at Lania's cocktail party,' I decided. 'Surely, after a few drinks, we ought to be able to guide the conversation around to poor John Blake and his sudden tragic death.'

Sixteen

It was a bright enough idea, but I'd overlooked a vital point: when we got to Lania's cocktail party, there was only one topic of conversation. That was what she had meant by 'the unveiling'.

I gasped as we crossed the threshold of the drawing-room. It had been redone completely. Instead of the cold, stark ice-floes, we stepped into a jungle. Deep lush green everywhere, leafy-patterned drapes and upholstery, bark-like furniture frames and tables like old tree stumps. Here and there, a splash of vivid colour denoted tropical blooms and sometimes actually were. I glanced down at my staid black dress with regret; I could have worn the crimson chiffon again and passed as a frangipani.

'Whew-ew!' Arnold whistled under his breath. 'All that's missing is the voodoo drums . . . and, maybe, the Earl of Greystoke.'

'Speaking of which – ' As my eyes became accustomed to the wild profusion, I began to pick out faces and forms. 'Look over there – behind the trailing vine.'

Lania, in a tropical white sleeveless dress and Piers, in pale tan trousers and safari jacket, were holding court at another oversized tree stump. They were dispensing drinks and greeting. All they lacked were pith helmets.

'Heh-heh – ' Arnold began and I nudged him sharply in the ribs. 'I could have worn my Bermuda shorts!' he gasped. We began edging our way over to Lania across the verdigreen and sludge swamp that was masquerading as a carpet – or vice versa.

'One gets so bored with things always being the same,' Lania was saying as we reached the jungle bar.

'It's certainly very dramatic,' a disembodied voice said. The effect was so uncanny that I blinked and looked hard in the direction of the voice. I found one of the neighbours who had been incautious enough to wear a green-patterned dress and thus had almost disappeared into the scenery.

We murmured our congratulations to Lania, collected our drinks, and retreated to the far side of the swamp.

'I don't see why she changed everything,' Arnold complained. 'And what did she do with all that other furniture?' His New England soul was affronted by conspicuous waste. 'It was all practically brand new.'

'Maybe it's your fault,' I said. 'You ruined her hedge out front, so she's moved all the greenery in here where you can't get at it again. There's probably some deep psychological – '

'Ah-hem . . .' There was a throat-clearing noise behind us. We turned to discover our putative host.

'Oh, Richard, I'd – ' I stopped short. I couldn't very well say, *I'd forgotten all about you*. Even though I had. Lania and Piers seemed so perfect a couple it was sometimes hard to remember that they weren't. Especially when they were engaged in the sort of double act they were doing now. Richard was the one who looked more out of place than some of the guests.

'Hi, Richard!' Arnold covered my lapse quickly. 'Never a dull moment, hey?'

'Well, hardly ever,' Richard murmured. He was leaning against the window frame, surveying the room with the air of a man who had builded his castle on shifting sands.

'It's pretty sensational,' Arnold went on, 'but I must admit I kinda liked the room the way it was before.'

'So did I.' Richard took a sip of his drink. 'And the way it was before that, and before that.' He shrugged. 'I'll get used to it, I suppose. I always do.'

'You mean this keeps on happening?' Arnold was stunned. He'd never believed me when I tried to tell him that other people redecorate their homes every decade or so, whether they need it or not.

'Ever since I was foolish enough to bring Piers home for dinner one evening and he joined our family circle.' Richard darted a baleful glare in the direction of the smooth blond head and writhed uncomfortably. He was wearing a T-shirt and tight blue jeans as his interpretation of what the well-dressed jungle explorer should wear. He had chosen wrong and he knew it. 'I should have worn a dinner jacket,' he muttered. 'Then I could be the stiff upper lipped sahib, keeping up the standards of civilization while the storm clouds gathered.'

'You look just fine,' I said unconvincingly. 'No one –' I stopped again. *No one is looking at you, anyway*, while true, could not be expected to be comforting.

'What happens – ?' Arnold returned to his original speculation. 'What happens to the furniture? This –'

he tapped the rough bark of a nearby chair – 'this isn't your old stuff recycled, is it?'

'Oh, no.' Richard shook his head and sipped again at his drink. I did not have the feeling that it was the drink that caused his lips to twist bitterly. 'Oh, no, we've turned a nice profit on the last lot. Don't worry about that. Piers brought some wealthy friends to tea last week, while I was at work. By sheer chance – ' his lips twisted again – 'they were doing up a new flat in Mayfair. They were so taken with the decor that – they took it. Very nice price. Allowed Lania and dear Piers to do all this and still have a nice profit left over.'

'It's really quite nice.' I tried to sound encouraging.

'Don't get too fond of it. It will only last until the next customer comes along. Sometimes, I think we should charge dear Piers a rental fee. We're saving him from paying for a showroom, after all. But I don't suppose Lania would wear it. She's quite content to let her family act as guinea pigs.'

Arnold and I exchanged glances. This wasn't going the way we had planned it. The room – or jungle clearing – was pretty crowded now. We hadn't realized it was going to be such a big party. Lania had made it sound as though just a few friends were dropping in. There were dozens of people we didn't know.

They all seemed to know each other, though, and were gathering in little cliques, backs turned to any outsiders. I was beginning to feel nearly as invisible as the woman in the green dress.

'Still, it's nice you made a profit.' Arnold turned back to Richard, who seemed the only one willing to carry on a conversation with us. Maybe because no one else was clamouring for his attention. An occasional cool nod was as much as he was accorded from people moving forward eagerly to speak to Lania and Piers. I began to suspect that this was a reception for his customers – past, present and potential. That would explain a lot of things.

'What did you do with the kids?' I asked. I could not imagine throwing a party without the twins underfoot. From an early age, they had learned to make themsleves useful by passing round the canapés and peanuts.

'They're upstairs,' Richard said. 'They live upstairs, poor little devils. They prefer it – and I don't blame them.'

'Children don't like change very much,' I agreed.

Richard gave a short bitter laugh, looked in surprise at his empty glass, and lurched away for a refill.

'Well,' Arnold said, 'do you think we ought to circulate?'

'We could try.' I looked at all the backs turned to us. 'But maybe we ought to finish our drinks first.'

'That's not a bad idea.' Arnold acted on it. 'Better than the last one you had. Or do you think any of these people knew John Blake? They don't seem to be locals – their accents are different.'

'I think this is a high-grade Tupperware party,' I said. 'Except that the furnishings are for sale instead of any smaller items.'

'You could be right.' Arnold looked sympathetic. 'Imagine having the furniture sold out from under you every time you turned around. It's enough to make a man wonder if he's in the right house if he comes home late at night.'

'Oh!' I spotted a familiar back. 'There's somebody we know!' Standing alone, her back to us, she was looking around uncertainly. She didn't seem to know anyone here, either.

'Hazel – ' I raised my voice above the crescendo of babbling voices. 'Here we are – come and join us. Hazel?'

Hazel moved off without even glancing round at us.

'Well! Well, how do you like that? She could at least have said hello.'

'Poor old Hazel – ' Richard had returned to us, bearing a full glass. 'Don't mind her. She does that every now and again. We think she's a bit deaf. One has to be facing her and speaking clearly. Otherwise, well, you saw her – ' He shrugged. 'We tried to joke with her about it once, but she got quite upset. It's obviously a sensitive subject. Go over and tap her on the shoulder. Once you've got her attention, she's all right. She concentrates then.'

'Okay.' I stalked Hazel across the swamp. She was walking aimlessly, obviously looking for familiar faces.

'Hazel – ' I tapped her on the shoulder, as instructed. She swung round to face me and broke into a wide smile. That was it, then, she hadn't meant to snub us, she just hadn't heard me. Not that it was too surprising anyway, the party was entering a very noisy stage.

'Hazel, we're over by the window.' I enunciated carefully. 'Come and join us.'

'Fine.' Her eyes carefully watching my lips, she

154

nodded. 'I'd love to. I was beginning to think I'd walked into the wrong party. I don't seem to know anyone here.'

'Neither do we. And when you add to that the fact that there's been a radical change in the decor – Well, if I hadn't seen Lania and Richard around, *I'd* have thought I was in the wrong house.'

'*And* Piers,' Hazel added absently. We twitched eyebrows at each other.

'Hazel, honey!' Arnold greeted her with an arm around her shoulder and a peck on the cheek. 'Great to see you!'

There was a slight stir in a nearby group and I became aware that one of the men had so far broken formation as to have turned and actually looked at us. At Arnold and Hazel – and there was an unpleasant look in his eyes.

'Er – ' I nudged Hazel and inclined my head towards the watcher. 'Who's your friend?'

'Never saw him before in my life.' She glanced at him just as he turned away – a bit too quickly to be casual. She frowned. 'Not that I recall,' she amended.

'Maybe he's a friend of your husband's – keeping an eye on you for him.' That would explain the disapproval at Arnold's gesture of affection.

'My husband has no friends.' She spoke without thinking; she had gone pale.

'Then he's a smart man,' Richard approved. His gaze wandered over our heads and found Piers. He had drunk just a bit too much and his stiff upper lip was in danger of wobbling. 'That way, he'll never get into trouble.'

'Oh, dear!' Hazel laughed nervously. 'I didn't mean

155

that the way it sounded. I just meant he doesn't have time to make friends, the way he's always travelling for the firm. Now that we've bought our house here, of course, we're planning to settle down and things will change.'

'Perhaps I ought to start travelling myself,' Richard murmured. 'Your husband can settle down here – and I'll take off. The swings and the roundabouts. Win some, lose some.'

'You don't want to do that,' I told him. 'You've already lost one good man around here. Look at John Blake.'

Okay, so I dragged the subject in by its heels and maybe I might have been more tactful about it. But how was I to know it would cause Hazel to burst into tears and run from the room?

Seventeen

'Oh-oh, you stepped on some toes there, honey,' Arnold said. 'I guess she still feels awful about it.'

Fortunately, nobody else seemed to notice, not even the man who had been glaring at us. The party was in full swing and people were interested only in their own little cliques. Those who weren't interested in Lania and Piers, that is.

There was quite a crowd around them now and it wasn't just because the bar was there. Piers was holding forth on some anecdote that was being hilariously received. Lania beamed beside him, interpolating small corrections to the story. They looked very intimate, very cosy, very much the host and hostess.

'It's always the wrong person who dies,' Richard brooded. 'Have you ever noticed?'

'You mean John Blake?' Arnold was deliberately obtuse. It was perfectly plain that Richard would have liked to have seen Piers drive over a cliff.

'Poor old John, poor devil. Everything to live for – and look what happened.'

'It's a tough world, all right,' Arnold sympathized.

'Terrible,' I agreed. 'A nice man like that. A man with no enemies . . .' I let the thought trail off, fishing.

'Wife who loved him . . . children who looked up

to him . . . everyone in town respected him. Man on his way up . . . might even have stood for Parliament some day. And won. No telling where he could have gone and – pffft! – over! Just like that.'

'A shame,' Arnold agreed. We dipped our heads in brief mourning while I tried to formulate the next leading question.

'*Other* men wouldn't even be missed – ' Richard's baleful gaze was fastened on Piers. 'Small loss to the world.'

Arnold and I looked at each other and remained silent. To agree, would have been to admit that the situation was becoming uncomfortably clear.

'Rosemary – ' I began, by way of getting back to the main subject. 'Rosemary must have been – '

'Especially me – ' Richard tossed down the last of his drink, still brooding over his wife and Piers. 'They'd never miss me.'

For a terrible moment, I thought there was going to be a real rooting-tooting scene. Then Richard turned back to us and smiled affably.

'Let me get you another drink.' He collected the glasses from our nerveless hands and headed for the tree stump bar.

'That was close, Babe,' Arnold said judiciously. 'That was very close, indeed.'

'That's what I thought.' We watched uneasily, but Richard merely handed the glasses to Lania to refill and waited beside her as she did so, neatly cutting her off from Piers and establishing his place at her side. Piers had the good sense to move away and begin mingling with his guests. 'But it's all blown over, I guess.'

'For this time, anyway,' Arnold said.

Richard seemed in no hurry to return to us; everybody else seemed intent on ignoring us. I'd had more fun at an Irish wake.

'I don't know about you, Arnold, but I feel a deep boredom setting in.'

'Me, too.' Arnold surreptitiously checked his watch. 'Do you think we can decently leave? We haven't been here very long.'

'It seems like hours.' Just then I felt something brush my ankles and muffled a shriek. I hadn't thought it was that kind of party. I sidestepped and glanced down. A familiar marmalade figure made a fresh assault on my ankles, twining round them.

'Esmond!' I swooped and caught him up. 'What are you doing here? Who let you in?'

'Never mind that,' Arnold said, chucking Esmond under the chin with approval. 'Here's our ticket out of here. We'll have to take him home.'

'Yes, we will, won't we?' I brightened. 'He must have slipped in when Hazel left. Clever Esmond, to find us in all this crowd.'

A couple of people standing nearby began smiling in our direction. Esmond was obviously more socially acceptable than we were. But it was too late, I just wanted to leave.

'You're not going?' Richard intercepted us at the door. 'I've just got your drinks.'

'Esmond sneaked in to join the party.' We accepted the drinks, since it seemed churlish not to, but continued edging towards the exit. 'We've got to take him home.'

'Ah, yes.' Richard patted Esmond's head absently.

'Not much for you at this party, Esmond. We usually have cocktail sausages, bits of cheese, things like that,' he explained. 'But this is a gathering of more serious drinkers. Lania decided just olives, nuts and Bombay mixture for them. Look on the bright side, Esmond – if they get drunk enough, someone may buy this jungle out from under us before we actually have to live in it.'

'Good luck on that, fella,' Arnold said.

'I live in hope.' Richard followed us to the front door. We drank hastily, trying to empty the glasses and escape before Esmond grew restive.

'If you get tired of all the foliage, come next door,' Arnold invited, 'and refresh your memory as to how the other half lives.'

'I might do that,' Richard agreed. 'By next week, I could have reached the breaking point.'

'That's stamina,' Arnold admired. 'I don't think I could hold out much past Saturday myself.'

'Ah, but that's only because I'll be away for a long weekend,' Richard said. 'I have a site inspection and conferences scheduled in Edinburgh. I may not get back until Monday or Tuesday; it depends how it goes.'

'Well – ' I drained my glass and set it down on the hall table – I think it was a hall table. 'Sorry to leave, but we've got to get this cat home. Thank you so much. It's been – '

'Please – ' He held up his hand, cutting me off in mid-lie. 'I quite understand. In fact, I quite agree.'

Although the party was a washout, Arnold was not deterred from his new project. The thought that

160

someone was gunning for him had concentrated his mind wonderfully.

'We'll have to go to direct sources,' he announced in the morning. Then amended, '*I'll* have to.'

'Arnold – ' I was immediately nervous. 'You can't go up and down the street with a notebook asking searching questions. The neighbours think we're crazy enough already.'

'Not *that* direct, honey. I mean records, reports, documents. All the stuff of history, only it's contemporary this time. Just a few months old – ' He could hardly contain his enthusiasm.

'Compared to my usual research, the printers' ink will still be wet on the documents. There are bound to be leads I can follow up – and the trail won't lead through dusty parchment and old books. It will lead to people with living memories, able to recount their stories in the flesh. It's a historian's dream – ' He came down to earth abruptly. 'Or, it would be, if it wasn't my neck on the chopping block.'

'You be careful, Arnold. If you think somebody's been trying to kill you just on general principles, what do you think they're going to do if they catch you snooping around like that?'

'Damned if I do – and damned if I don't.' Arnold's face tightened with a new determination. 'If I have to go down, I'm going down fighting!'

'Who are you fighting, Dad?' Donald came into the kitchen, Donna just behind him. 'Are you gonna get those guys who beat you up?'

'Never you mind,' Arnold said. 'Sit down and eat your breakfast.'

161

'You're late, Daddy,' Donna worried. 'You're going to miss your train.'

'He's already missed it,' Donald said. 'What's the next train? Shall I get the timetable?'

'Never mind,' Arnold said again. 'I'm not going up to London today. I'm going to, er, work locally for a few days.'

'Will you be home to lunch every day, then?' My practical Donna produced a question that had not yet crossed my mind. I waited with interest for the answer.

'I might be – ' Arnold caught my eye and grinned suddenly. 'On the other hand, I might come home every day and take us all out to lunch. How about that? There are a lot of nice-looking places around here that we haven't tried.'

'That's one of your better ideas,' I told him. 'Starting today, I hope?'

'Why not? I'll begin at the library this morning and see how much they've got on file. When I've exhausted their resources, I'll move on to the local newspaper. They might even have some back copies to sell me so that I can study them at home.'

That routine worked very well, right through to Saturday. To tell the truth, I was relieved to be able to keep a closer eye on Arnold – and not just for the lovely luncheons at country inns. Nothing else dire happened and I was gradually losing my conviction that he was the designated victim of some mad murderer – who would have to be mad to want to kill poor, innocent Arnold. But I was happier not having him disappear up to London every day, never knowing what condition he might be in when he returned. If he returned. No, a discreet check on his condition over a lunch somebody else had cooked and served suited me very well.

It kept the twins happy, too. The only snag was that we couldn't carry on much of a conversation with them around. We solved that by sending them upstairs early every evening to watch television while we retreated to the study to discuss Arnold's discoveries of the day, if any.

All in all, Arnold and I hadn't spent so much time alone together since the early days of our marriage. I began to remember why I had fallen in love with him. He could be very good company – when you got him out of his libraries and away from his dusty old records.

He was looking better these days, too, despite his injuries. The enforced rest had relaxed him, he had lost a certain amount of flabbiness since he had been so active catching trains and buses; most of all, a new sense of purpose had hardened his jaw and tightened his muscles.

'Penny for your thoughts, Babe.'

Also, he was paying more attention to me. A few weeks ago, back in New Hampshire, he would never have noticed whether or not I was thinking anything.

'I was just thinking you're quite a guy.' Then, so as not to spoil him, I added. 'In your own way, that is.'

'You wouldn't swap me, then? Not even for Piers?'

'Especially not for Piers. Richard, now . . .' I dodged a mock blow, laughing.

'Lania's crazy.' Arnold sobered suddenly. 'Messing

163

around a nice guy like Richard. I wouldn't blame him if he didn't put up with it any longer.'

'Do you really think she's seriously involved?'

'Would you let some guy use your living-room as an out-of-town showroom, if you *weren't* seriously involved?'

'Well, no, but this is England. Things may be different here.'

'Not *that* different.' Arnold rubbed his wounded arm reflectively. 'I'd call it more than serious. I'd call it blatant. And I wouldn't blame Richard if he did a bit of murdering on his own account.'

'Lania's so silly. She's got everything: a lovely home, a good husband, two nice children, and – ' I looked at the piles of photocopies and back-issue newspapers on the desk. 'And she's got Rosemary's example. She's seen how easily it can all be swept away. Even at the best of times, life is so precarious. Why should she risk everything she's got?'

'Some women never believe it can happen to them.' He looked at me sombrely. 'Even you don't, do you, Babe? Not down deep?'

'I don't want to.'

'Yet it happened to the Blakes.' He rifled one of the piles of photocopies. 'There's the collected evidence. We'll begin sifting through it tomorrow. Maybe we'll find a clue somewhere in there.'

'Maybe.' I clung to my doubt. I didn't want to believe that Arnold could be in mortal danger. Yet, all those strange things had been happening . . .

'Let's get a good night's sleep.' Arnold turned off the desk light. 'We'll come to the problem fresh in the morning.'

Eighteen

The twins were in bed and peacefully sleeping, which was more than we could manage. I lay awake, trying not to mind that I was occupying a dead man's bed; trying not to think how swiftly Rosemary's happiness had been swept away; trying not to believe that someone – for some unknown reason – might be planning to do the same to Arnold and me. I tried to lie quietly and not disturb Arnold. He was restless himself, however, and kept tossing and turning.

'Sorry, honey,' he muttered. 'Maybe I should have taken the sofa in the study so as not to disturb you. It's this damned arm – every time I'm almost asleep, it feels as though they're pulling the stitches out all over again and I jump awake.'

'It's all right,' I said. 'Just breathe deeply and count sheep, or something.'

Maybe we actually dozed off for a bit, unlikely though it seemed. The next thing I was aware of was that peculiar silence the dead of night brings. No traffic, no sounds of human life anywhere; just the occasional hum of machinery carrying on a hidden malevolent existence of its own in some secret subterranean depths.

Then I heard a noise that was all too human. I blinked into wakefulness.

'Arnold . . .?' I whispered uncertainly. 'Are you all right?'

There was a low passionate groan.

'Gee, honey,' Arnold mumbled. 'I'm sorry. I'm just too bushed. Can't you take a raincheck?'

'Arnold,' I said. 'That wasn't me. Wasn't it you?'

'Hell no!' Arnold sounded more alert. 'Maybe the kids are watching a late night television film.'

'Television closed down for the night hours ago.'

I saw a circle of tiny fluorescent numbers sweep through the air as Arnold groped for his watch and brought it into focus. 'You're right,' he said. 'It's two a.m.'

There came a long languorous sigh.

'*That* wasn't me! It wasn't you – and it sure as hell wasn't Esmond!' I heard the thump as Arnold's feet hit the floor, then the bedside lamp flashed on.

'Arnold – ' My eyes closed in protest against the sudden blaze of light. I felt disorientated, far from home – and frightened. Everything I had ever read about Borley Rectory, headless coachmen, walled-up nuns, and all the dead but ever-present inhabitants of Olde England paraded through my mind. 'Arnold – you don't suppose the house is haunted, do you? Do you think we have ghosts?'

A very earthly chuckle suddenly answered me, jolting my eyes wide open. The bedroom was just the same, ordinary, familiar – and yet, there was someone in it with us.

'It came from over there – ' Arnold advanced grimly on the farther wall. 'There's something funny going on here,' he said.

'Arnold, come back to bed. We can investigate in

the morning.' If we were being disturbed by spirits, I didn't want to know about it. 'Maybe we ought to go to church – and see what the parson's feelings are about exorcism ceremonies.'

'There's a rational explanation, Babe,' Arnold assured me. 'There *has* to be.'

I wasn't so sure, but I wasn't going to wait alone in that big bed while Arnold antagonized the forces of darkness. I groped my way into my dressing gown and crept over to stand behind him. 'Don't wake the twins,' I begged.

He didn't even hear me. He was prowling along the wall, face intent, head cocked to pick up any sound from the lath and plaster.

'Please, Arnold, come back to bed.'

'Presently, presently . . .' He tapped experimentally at the inner wall. I don't know why – he'd have no more idea than I would whether the right sound was bouncing back at him.

But the quality of the noise echoing through the room changed. An uneasy puzzled note crept into it.

'Funny . . .' Arnold rapped the wall again. 'Sounds hollow back there.'

'Oh, my God!' Suddenly, it came to me. 'Arnold that's the wall between the two halves of the house. You're banging on Lania's bedroom wall.'

'The noise is coming from there,' Arnold said stubbornly, just before the enormity of his behaviour dawned on him. 'We've never heard anything from there before.'

'Maybe the wind has changed, or something.' I caught at his pyjama sleeve. 'Arnold, forget it –'

'And Richard is away for the weekend –' Arnold

167

continued plodding along the one track his sleep-drugged mind was presenting. 'What's all this white stuff around the bookcase?'

'I don't know.' I hadn't noticed the fine white powder ground into the carpet until he mentioned it. But then, I'd been too busy to read lately. 'Arnold, let's just go back to bed and forget it – '

'Take hold of the other end of the bookcase, honey. Let's shift it a bit. Maybe there's a disused chimney behind there, or something.'

'Arnold, this is against my better judgement – ' But there was no use arguing with him. He was heaving at his side of the bookcase and he'd only give himself a hernia or a slipped disc if I didn't help. Reluctantly, I grasped the edge nearest me.

'This would be a lot easier if we took the books out of it first.'

'It's coming, honey. You're doing fine.'

Gradually, the bookcase swung out from the wall. I was concentrating on keeping it steady so that we didn't get an avalanche of books into the room, waking the twins, when:

'Christ!' Arnold exclaimed. 'What the hell – ?'

That was when I looked at the wall – or what should have been the wall – and screamed.

I couldn't help it. It was a reflex action. There was no wall there!

There were the remains of a wall – around the edges of a great gaping hole, almost a second doorway. Strips of wallpaper, raw plaster, and brick formed an arc opening on to the unfinished wooden back of a piece of bedroom furniture.

Even as we gaped at it, the dressing table was

wrenched away and we stood facing the people on the other side of the hole.

This time, it was Lania who screamed. Piers, standing immediately behind her and clutching a slipping duvet around himself, seemed dumbstruck.

'What the hell is going on here?' Arnold demanded.

'That's just what I'd like to know.' Lania got a firmer grip on her dressing gown, but not before I had been able to see that she wore nothing underneath it. 'What have you done to my wall – and why? Even if you *are* voyeurs, you seem to be carrying it to extraordinary lengths!'

'Now wait just a minute – ' Arnold began.

'Try waiting yourself!' Piers stepped forward menacingly and we had a few moments of confused uproar.

'Hold it!' I put up my hand, silencing everyone momentarily, and leaned forward to get a better view into Lania's bedroom. In the distance, two small pale faces had appeared briefly before withdrawing. It was a definite indication of guilty knowledge. I whirled abruptly to catch my own two in the process of a swift retreat.

'Donna! Donald! Come back here!' I ordered.

There was a long thoughtful pause before they reluctantly obeyed. Meanwhile, I leaned forward again and raised my voice.

'Angela! Peregrine! We saw you. Come here this instant!'

'What?' Lania turned to the doorway on the far side of the room. Piers readjusted his duvet inadequately and took a few steps back.

'Hurry up!' I insisted.

Slowly, they crept forward. So did the twins, until they stood each on their own side of the hacked-out aperture. They looked at each other warily, trying to communicate caution in the face of the adult enemy.

Suddenly, it all fell into place: the way the twins had been quoting Angela and Peregrine – even though they had been confined to quarters and incommunicado for the past week. Even Esmond's sudden appearance at the party last night was explained – he hadn't slipped in when Hazel left, he'd found his way through the bedroom wall. And no wonder he'd been so upset when I accused him of slacking – there'd been no mice here for him to catch.

'Okay, you kids,' I said. 'Start talking.'

'Isn't it great?' Donald tried to brazen it out. 'If those soccer hooligans ever come after Dad again, we've got an escape hatch for him. He can just disappear behind the bookcase and get away.'

'We got the idea from television.' Peregrine appeared to feel that this explanation sanctified their endeavour. 'From *The Wooden Horse*. You know, when the prisoners of war tunnelled their way to freedom – '

'*You* – ' Lania was shaking with fury. 'You ripped our house apart because of a television programme?'

'And you carried out the chunks of plaster and debris in your pockets,' I accused the twins. It was all coming clear to me. 'And in your shoes. *That* was why you were limping – it wasn't blisters, at all. You were lying, too!' I was fighting to control myself, but I was even more furious than Lania.

The twins cringed. Arnold put a restraining hand on my shoulder, but I shook it off.

'This is monstrous!' Lania raged. 'A nightmare!' She glared across the opening at us. 'My children would never have dreamed of doing such a thing if it weren't for your undisciplined brats! They're the worst possible influence and – '

'Now hold it right there!' I snapped. 'Mine could never have thought up such an idea by themselves. It was your little rays of sunshine who knew the layout of the house. If you hadn't been too busy alley-catting around to pay the proper attention to them – '

'I think we'd better sleep on this.' Arnold pulled me back into our room. 'We can discuss it in the morning like civilized people. We can't do anything about it at the moment, and arguing isn't going to get us anywhere.'

'An excellent idea.' Piers moved forward tentatively and grasped Lania's arm. She shook him off. His duvet began slipping again. He was trying his best, but it was too bulky to drape like a Roman toga.

'Mummy – ' Angela piped up innocently – 'what's alley-catting?'

'Mummy – ' Peregrine was also swift to the defensive attack – 'what's Uncle Piers doing here so late? And why is he wearing a duvet?'

Those kids were going to be able to take care of themselves. They'd probably had plenty of practice.

Lania lashed out. Her hand connected with tiny ears and the air was filled with soul-satisfying howls.

For once, I was in total agreeement with Lania. I turned grimly towards the twins. They began edging away.

'Honey – ' Arnold tried to restrain me. 'Honey, let's leave it until morning – '

'Shut up, Arnold!' I advanced on the twins and did some lashing out of my own. Fresh howls rent the air.

'I say, old man – ' Piers called across to Arnold. 'I think we ought to leave this to the ladies and do something more practical ourselves. Shall we move the furniture back into position and call it a night? As you say, we can begin sorting things out in the cold, clear light of day.'

'Good idea.' Arnold began tugging at the bookcase. He straightened abruptly as a new thought hit him. 'I suppose these houses are insured?'

'Bound to be, old man. Mind you, I don't know what category this sort of damage would fall under. Act of God, perhaps? . . . No, perhaps not . . .'

'Maybe you'd better find the insurance policy and check it out – ' Arnold paused, another unwelcome thought hitting him. 'I mean, maybe Richard had better.'

'Quite so.' Piers looked across at him uneasily. 'Perhaps we ought to have a council of war in the morning . . . get all our stories straight.'

Nineteen

Morning eventually dawned, so dark and wet it was barely distinguishable from the night. Nearly as black as my mood, in fact. Another jolly day in Merrie England, fraught with danger and peril for all concerned. Especially my nearest and dearest. I could hear the twins shuffling about in the hallway outside, hungry for their breakfast but nervous about coming in and facing me. They were right.

'Why don't we tell Richard — ?' Arnold poured himself another cup of coffee. 'Tell Richard that Lania was having a nightmare — and that was how come we heard her? She cried out in her sleep.' He was warming to his story. 'She cried out several times — it was a really bad nightmare. We heard her and started investigating — and that was how we found out what had happened to the wall.'

'Why don't we just tell Richard the truth?' I asked coldly. 'It will hardly come as any surprise to him.'

'Oh, now, honey, we want to try to keep this respectable — '

'I fail to see why *we* should worry about Lania's respectability when *she* doesn't.' Since he was pouring, I held out my cup for more coffee. I'd already had too much and it would probably give me a first-class case of caffeine jitters, but who cared? I'd had little enough sleep last night; now I needed to keep awake.

'I think Richard has enough problems without our adding to them.' Arnold had a point there, but I was in too bad a mood to concede it.

'We've all got problems.'

'You're right.' Arnold's mind flew to his own problem. 'I wanted to spend the day going through my research.' He looked yearningly towards the study. 'Only now we've got to try to sort out this mess.' His own mood was visibly worsening and I watched him with gloomy satisfaction.

There were louder scuffling noises from the hall. Arnold was diverted.

'Was that the kids?' he asked. 'Don't they want to come in?'

'Not if they're smart — ' I raised my voice. 'If they're smart, they'll run away from home.'

'Aw, honey, don't be like that. It was just a childish escapade.'

'Oh, yes. And do you have any idea how much that childish escapade is likely to cost us?'

'Good morning, Dad . . .' The twins sidled into the kitchen, wearing their best hangdog expressions. 'Good morning, Mom . . .'

'What's good about it?' I eyed them coldly, wondering what the penalty was for infanticide over here. No, make that justifiable homicide.

'We're sorry, Mom,' Donna said. She exchanged glances with her twin and, as though on cue, they both hunched their shoulders and looked pathetic. 'We're awfully sorry.'

'We didn't — ' Donald offered the formula that had

174

often led to forgiveness before. Unfortunately for
him, it was the wrong thing to say this time. 'We
didn't mean it.'

'You didn't mean it? *You didn't mean it*? How can
you tear down half a wall – and NOT MEAN IT?'

'Take it easy, honey,' Arnold soothed. The twins
backed away from my fury and began to cry.

'How can I take it easy? It's all right for you to talk
– but I'm the one who's going to have to write to
Rosemary Blake and try to explain. What can I say to
that poor wretched woman? She's lost her husband –
and now we've torn her home to pieces!'

'Honey – '

'Don't Honey me!' I sobbed. 'I can't do it. I can't
write one more grovelling letter apologizing for
having whelped a couple of lousy vandals instead of
human beings!'

'It was Perry's idea,' Donald whined defensively.
'We were watching *The Wooden Horse* and he said
we could make an escape tunnel of our own. Only
through the wall, instead of underground. Angela did
a lot of digging, too.'

'Oh, great, great! That explains everything! And, if
they'd wanted to blow up Buckingham Palace because
they saw somebody do it on television, would you
have gone along with that, too?'

'We didn't mean – ' Donna began, then abruptly
remembered that that was a dangerous plea to cop.
'We're sorry,' she snivelled. 'We – we'll pay for it.
You can deduct it from our allowance.'

'You should live so long!' The kitchen was beginning to tilt alarmingly. I took a firm grip on the edge
of the table.

'Honey –' Arnold said warningly.

'You're right about one thing,' I told them. 'It's going to be a long time before you see your allowance again. And it will be a cold day in hell before you watch any more television. Arnold, go upstairs and unplug their set! Bring it down here and throw it in the study for the time being.'

'No –' Donna squealed. I was hitting them where it really hurt. 'Please, Mom, we'll be good –'

'Mom! Hey, Mom –' Donald protested. 'It wasn't *our* fault – not *all* of it!'

'Don't worry,' I said. 'I'm going to have an in-depth conversation with Lania this afternoon. Angela and Peregrine aren't going to be watching television for a long time, either. It's going to be back to tiddlywinks for the lot of you!'

I was just barely conscious of their cries of anguish as the world went black.

When I came to, I was lying on the sofa in the study. The world slowly moved back into focus. Arnold was sitting in the wing chair, reading a newspaper. Water dripped from the hedge outside and beat against the window panes. I shifted position and moaned.

'Feeling better, honey?' Arnold laid aside his paper and struggled out of his chair. 'Sorry we had to put you in here, but I couldn't carry you up to bed. Even with the twins helping, I couldn't manage – and I didn't think you'd want me to go next door for help.'

'You were so right.' I heaved myself up on one elbow and squinted towards the windows. The quality of light seemed not to have changed at all. What time is it?'

'Nearly lunch time,' Arnold said promptly. 'You went from fainting to sleeping with barely a murmur, so we didn't disturb you. Donna's peeling the potatoes now and Donald's scraping carrots. The kids have been great, honey. Very supportive, all morning.'

'I'm *so* glad.' He winced at my tone – and he was right to. 'It's about time they began to do something *con*structive, rather than *de*structive.'

'I've talked to Lania,' he said quickly, 'and we've postponed our conference until this evening. You can take it easy all afternoon. You need some rest.'

'I sure do.' I closed my eyes again and fell back against the cushions. I was feeling better, but not prepared to admit it. Let them worry about me for a change – turn about was fair play.

Then I heard the sound of pages turning and opened my eyes. Arnold had resumed his seat and gone back to his newspapers. He was still worrying more about himself than about me.

'Have you found anything?' I asked, giving up.

'Not a thing.' He gestured hopelessly to the pile of newspapers at his feet. 'According to all this, John Blake was the original Mr Clean. Everything's there: the account of the accident, the police search for the other driver, the report of the funeral, tributes from colleagues, the obituary, letters from people he'd helped. One of the Nice Guys of the world – no reason anyone could possibly have for murdering him. And yet, he's dead.'

'Maybe it *was* an accident.'

'Then why is it still going on? Why is it aimed at me? I can't figure out any rhyme or reason for it, except that I'm square in the target area.'

177

'In that case, we're in the target area, too – the kids and me. So why haven't they tried to hurt us?'

'You were in the car with me when it went out of control.'

'Yes, but nothing has happened to us since. And there've been two more attempts on your life. Also – Lania and Richard are in the target area – and nothing's happened to them. That can't be the answer, Arnold. It doesn't make sense.'

'Maybe not,' he sighed. 'I've been clinging to it because the only other answer I can think of is even more frightening: somebody's taken out a contract on me.'

'Arnold!' I wanted to say that such things didn't happen, only there were more reports of them happening every day. But – to people like us? 'Why? Who would do such a thing?'

'I wish I knew. I've never done anything worse than fail a few lousy students who deserved it. Some of their parents got pretty mad – but I don't think they were *that* mad. Besides, nothing ever happened to me in New Hampshire. They'd have done it there, if they wanted revenge. They couldn't chase me all the way over here.'

'A contract . . .' I shuddered. 'Arnold, that's awful. It's – it's so impersonal. That means it could be anybody doing it. While the person who gave the orders stays hundreds of miles away with a perfect alibi.'

'That's about the size of it, honey. It needn't even have cost them very much. For sure, there wouldn't have been much problem about getting those soccer hooligans to kick me around. They'd probably have done it for nothing. If somebody slipped them a few big ones and suggested they give their knives a workout, too, it would have been money for jam to them.'

'Arnold — let's get out of here!' I threw back the coverlet and leaped to my feet. 'We don't have to hang around here and — and wait for somebody to kill you! We can catch a flight back to the States in the morning. On standby. If there aren't enough seats, you can get away first and the kids and I will follow you. We'll rent a cottage for the rest of the summer until Rosemary leaves our house. I'll start packing —'

'It's no good, Babe.' He caught me as I dashed for the door. 'How do we know that would stop them? Whatever it is, we may be in too deep.'

'Oh, God!' I let him lead me back to the sofa. 'How did we get into this?'

'If we knew, we wouldn't have gotten into it. That is, *I* wouldn't have.' He went back to the desk and picked up another pile of newspapers. 'I've already been through these —' He put them down beside me. 'Suppose you have a look. You might spot something I've missed.'

'How can I spot anything when I don't know what we're looking for?' It kept coming back to that. I lifted the top paper listlessly and scanned meaningless headlines. It was dated a lot earlier than the accident and had the usual London-based reports of criminal and spy trials at the Old Bailey, complete with the inevitable supergrasses and weeping mothers who claimed their dear sweet sons could never have done such awful things and all the evidence had been rigged against them. Just like the Stateside trials and the inevitable refrain: 'We was framed.'

Arnold had evidently bought that issue because there was a small story buried in the inner pages about the Blake children winning some prizes at a local Riding Academy. I wondered if it might be a good idea to enrol the twins in something like that so that they could work off their surplus energy and keep out of mischief. If we stayed here much longer, that is.

'Arnold,' I said, 'I still think we ought to leave the country. It's worth a try.'

'I don't like running away.' Arnold's jaw set stubbornly. 'You and the kids can go, if you like – '

'Not without you!' He was the reason I wanted to get out of here; to get him to safety.

'I haven't scratched the surface of my research yet – ' He caught my eye and realized that this was a dangerous excuse to give me.

'Besides – ' he added hastily – 'we can't just walk out and leave the house in the condition it's in now. We'll have to repair the damage first.'

Twenty

Lania accepted a drink from Arnold and leaned back comfortably on the sofa, quite as though this were an ordinary social occasion. You had to hand it to her for nerve.

Piers was rather more conscious that a certain constraint hung in the air. He retreated with his drink to a chair some distance from Lania. A bit late for that.

'Come here, Piers.' She seemed to think so, too. She patted the place beside her. Reluctantly, he joined her on the sofa.

Arnold took the armchair across from them and I perched on the arm. There was an awkward silence. Arnold and Piers bared their teeth at each other. Lania and I didn't bother.

'The way I see it — ' Arnold began, just as Piers said:

'I *do* think — '

They stopped and apologized to each other.

'I'm sure we're all agreed,' Lania said smoothly, 'that we want that wall repaired as quickly as possible. Speed is of the essence.'

This time, I did bare my teeth. I didn't blame her for trying, but there was no way she was going to get that wall rebuilt before her husband got home. Then we were both going to have to re-wallpaper the bedrooms and I doubted that Lania had kept any spare rolls.

'I could make a start on it – ' Arnold offered.

'Oh no you don't!' I said quickly and explained to the others. 'Any time Arnold tries do-it-yourselfing, he creates an area of Urban Blight for the next twenty years!'

'I'll bring my people in,' Piers said. 'They can do your side, as well, if you like.'

'That would be more sensible,' I agreed.

'Of course, I'll have to pull them off another job – '

I looked at him incredulously. Was he going to start bargaining?

'We thought we'd say we heard Lania having a nightmare – ' Arnold offered. That effectively reminded them that they were in no position to bargain. 'And *that* was how we came to discover what had happened to the wall.'

'Er, yes.' Piers flushed slightly. 'Good idea.'

'How about the insurance policy?' Arnold turned to Lania. 'Have you checked it?'

'I don't know where Richard keeps it,' Lania said. 'He'll take care of all that when he gets home tomorrow or Tuesday. We can have a proper discussion then. Meanwhile, it would be best to authorize that the work be put in hand immediately.'

'That's okay by us – '

The doorbell rang, cutting Arnold off.

'It must be your kids – ' I hazarded a guess.

'It couldn't be,' Lania said. 'We left them watching television. They wouldn't leave their programme.'

182

'You still let them watch television – after what they've done?'

'They didn't do it alone!' she snapped, then recovered and smiled sweetly. 'It's a programme they especially wanted to see. I didn't want to deny them – when the whole episode wasn't entirely their fault.'

'Oh, sure.' I went to answer the door. I had forgotten – but Angela and Peregrine hadn't – that Lania was eminently blackmailable from now on. There wasn't going to be much she'd be able to deny the little darlings in the future.

I opened the door to find Esmond at eye level. I was so startled it took me a moment to look up and discover who was holding him. Then I nearly went into deep shock.

'Richard! What are you doing home? We weren't expecting you until tomorrow or Tuesday.'

'Obviously.' He swept past me grimly, still clutching Esmond, and headed unerringly for the living-room. As I closed the door and followed him, I saw that he was also carrying a suitcase.

'Good evening, everyone.' He nodded curtly to his wife and former colleague, then turned to Arnold. 'I wanted to return your cat,' he said. 'Esmond seems to think he's found a very superior cat flap installed just for his benefit. I met him strolling out from behind the dressing table and investigated.'

'Oh, Richard,' Lania said, 'I'm sorry. I was going to break it to you gently.'

'Well, there you are. Nothing like an animal for giving the game away. I suppose, if he'd been a dog, he'd have fetched my slippers and – ' he smiled at Piers dangerously – 'delivered them to you.'

'Esmond, darling!' I swooped over and collected him. 'How naughty of you – ' It was a good try, but I knew instinctively that it wasn't going to avert the storm.

'We're awfully sorry,' Arnold said. 'We wouldn't have had this happen for the world, but the kids – '

'Yes, I know,' Richard said. 'The children told me.' It was quite clear that that was not all they had told him.

'You're back early.' Lania was still trying to preserve a smooth social surface. 'Were your conferences cancelled?'

'They were never scheduled,' he said. 'I thought it was about time we brought this to a head.'

'I think we should go home – ' Lania rose to her feet.

'Why? I don't think Nancy and Arnold can have any illusions left after last night.' Richard turned to us. 'Have you?'

'Poor Esmond must be starving,' I said quickly. 'I'll take him out in the kitchen and feed him.'

'I'll help you.' Arnold lurched to his feet.

'I was just leaving – ' Piers got up and moved hastily towards the exit.

'Don't let me spoil your weekend,' Richard told Piers coldly. 'I haven't unpacked. I thought – ' he looked at Arnold – 'you might be able to put me up for a night or two, while I look around for something else? I know your sofa opens into a bed.'

'Oh, sure,' Arnold said. 'Sure. Glad to have you – I mean, it's okay with us. Stay as long as you like.'

'Thank you.' Richard deposited his suitcase in a corner.

'Richard, don't be absurd,' Lania said. 'Come home and we'll settle this quietly.'

'It's too late,' he said. 'I thought I could trust you to be discreet, at least. But now –'

'That isn't fair!' I spoke without thinking. 'How could anybody be discreet with their bedroom wall missing?'

Arnold sunk his elbow into my ribs and hustled me towards the kitchen. I didn't object. Even Esmond seemed glad to get out of that room.

We hung around in the kitchen until we heard the front door slam. It seemed to take a long while. After the silence had gone on for some time, we went back to the living-room, hoping for the best. We didn't get it. Lania and Piers had left, but Richard was still there.

Still there – and making himself at home. He had pulled the sofa out, turning it into a bed, and unpacked his pyjamas. Well, we *had* said he could stay. There was nothing to do but put the best face on it.

'Let me get you a drink,' Arnold said.

'Thanks, I could use one.'

I went round the room and collected the empty glasses. It didn't seem tactful to have them cluttering up the place – and reminding us of the people who had so recently been drinking from them.

'I think we ought to tell him, honey,' Arnold said, as I returned empty-handed from the kitchen. 'He might be able to help us.'

'Tell me?' Richard asked nervously. 'What more is there?' He had the nerve-racked look of a man who has been told: 'That was the good news, now for the bad.'

'Somebody,' I said, 'is trying to murder Arnold.'

'Oh,' Richard breathed a sigh of relief. 'Is that – ?' He broke off abruptly, obviously having realized that *Is that all*? was not quite the comment called for.

'Truly,' I said.

'What makes you think so?' Richard was intrigued rather than convinced.

'All those accidents I've been having,' Arnold said. 'Don't they make you think?'

'Hmmm . . .' Richard said non-committally.

'The brakes *could* have failed,' Arnold said. 'But didn't it strike you as too much of a coincidence that a gang of soccer hooligans should set on me when I was minding my own business at the other end of the station from them?'

'I hadn't thought of that,' Richard said soothingly – too soothingly. He was humouring Arnold.

'And somebody deliberately tried to push me under that bus,' Arnold wound up his case. 'I *felt* that shove. No way could it have been an accident. Somebody's out to get me!'

'Why?' Richard asked simply. It was an excellent question. One we had not been able to answer.

'Not only that – ' I leaped in, avoiding the question. 'We'd like to know more about John Blake's death. In view of what's been happening to Arnold, it strikes us as highly suspicious!'

'That's insane!' Richard shook his head dazedly. 'I mean – ' He remembered his manners – and that he was our guest for the night and perhaps several nights to come. 'I mean, there was never any question about

186

that. It was an accident. The Coroner's Inquest said so.'

'It's true!' All I had needed to convince me of that truth was a bit of opposition. 'Arnold is in desperate danger of his life. They killed John Blake – now they're trying to kill Arnold, too! You've got to help us. You know Blake's background. There must be something in it somewhere that will explain all this.'

'Er, yes, certainly.' Richard looked profoundly uncomfortable. 'I'll, er, do all I can . . . er, to help.' Now he was humouring both of us.

'I know it sounds incredible – ' Arnold had caught Richard's longing look towards his own half of the house; he was quite obviously having second thoughts about spending the night with a pair of lunatics. 'We've sprung it on you too quickly. We should have led up to it gradually – '

'No, no,' Richard murmured, edging away. 'Quite all right. Er, as you say, it's a bit sudden. I dare say I'll get used to the idea.'

'Just think about it,' I urged. 'I didn't believe it at first, either.'

'But it doesn't make sense,' Richard protested mildly, still cautious about upsetting us. 'There's no reason in the world why anyone should have wanted to kill . . . John Blake.' I noticed he wasn't so certain about Arnold.

'How well did you know Blake – *really* know him?' I was growing desperate. Here we had somebody who might have the key to the mystery hidden away in some recess of his brain, in his knowledge of background and events before we had appeared on the scene – and he was balking. He wasn't taking it seriously.

'Please, please,' I begged. '*Think*! There *must* be something, somewhere. Maybe just some tiny thing that didn't ring true at the time . . . something you noticed but forgot again . . . something you don't even *know* you know . . .

'Please – ' I was close to tears. I felt like the beleaguered heroine in some old film, pleading for her lover's life while the mood music swelled in the background. 'You *must* believe us. Arnold's *life* is at stake!'

There was deep silence from Richard, while the orchestra soared in a crescendo . . .

Wait a minute – there *was* an orchestra playing in the background!

'God damn it!' I exploded. 'Those brats have sneaked down to the study and are watching television again!'

Richard flinched. For a moment, I'd almost had him convinced. Now he was back to thinking we were crazy again.

'Shhh!' I held up my hand. 'We'll catch them in the act – ' I tiptoed over to the study door and eased it open silently.

It was a black and white movie, with all the moody shades of grey that established foreboding and dread. The music throbbed softly.

In the middle of the screen, a man lifted bandaged hands to his bandaged head and slowly began unwinding the bandages – upon emptiness.

'See – ' Donald nudged his sister. 'I told you. She had a date with the Invisible Man!'

'Okay, you kids – ' I snapped on the light abruptly, but my anger had disappeared, driven out by a new thought. 'Suppose you explain.'

'We only wanted to watch for a few minutes – just this part.' Donald was frightened by my expression.

'Just this one movie – ' Donna began to sniffle. 'We won't do it again.'

'Never mind that – ' I snapped the television off. 'I want to know what you meant about the Invisible Man – it's not the first time you've made that crack. Was that what you saw in Boulogne?' I waved towards the darkened screen. 'Hazel, meeting a man in bandages?'

'Well . . .' Donald said carefully, not understanding what this was about, but grateful that I had been deflected from the major issue of their deliberate disobedience. 'Well, his *hands* weren't bandaged.'

'But his head was?'

'His face,' Donna corrected. 'It wasn't an all-around bandage, like that. I guess they'd never have let him out of the hospital these days, if it was. But there were bandages all over his face – and he had dark glasses over his eyes.'

'Okay!' I threw discipline to the winds. 'You can go back to watching the movie. It's a good one. Very illuminating.' I withdrew back into the living-room and closed the door behind me.

'What is it, Babe?' Arnold studied my face anxiously. 'What's the matter?'

'I was just thinking,' I said slowly. 'Maybe we've been approaching this from the wrong angle. Maybe we shouldn't have been worrying about John Blake's past at all. Maybe he was just an innocent bystander . . . like Arnold.'

'What do you mean?' Richard was caught by my tone.

'Think about it – ' My mind was travelling like lightning in a dozen different directions – all converging on the same point. 'John Blake died after he'd spent a couple of hours with Hazel. Then, the first attack on Arnold occurred after *he'd* been alone with Hazel for a couple of hours. The next attack was after he'd been snuggling up to her in public, right under her porch light – '

'I wasn't snuggling up,' Arnold protested. 'It was just a friendly hug – '

'And the third attack was after that day trip to Boulogne, when Arnold boarded the bus with Hazel, looking very chummy.'

'You told me not to wait while you parked – '

'And now we find out that Hazel met a strange man in Boulogne – after she'd told us she was going to a dressmaker for fittings. A man in bandages.

'I don't know how it seems to you – ' I looked from Arnold to Richard – 'but it strikes me that any man who spends much time around Hazel has a pretty rough time. She ought to carry a Government warning: she's more hazardous to health than high-tar cigarettes!'

Twenty One

'Hello – ?' The voice at the other end of the phone was wary. It was late at night and any woman had a right to feel uneasy about a sudden unexpected call. I wondered if Hazel had special reason to fear. A wildly jealous husband, perhaps?

'Hazel,' I said quickly, 'it's Nancy Harper. I'm sorry to be ringing so late, but I wanted to catch you before you made too many plans for the children – '

'Plans?' She sounded surprised. 'For the twins?'

'No, not *my* children,' I said. '*Yours*. The school holidays have started. You'll have them home again. I wanted to – '

'Oh, no,' she said. 'No, I won't! They – they've gone to their grandparents . . . in Wales. It seemed better – I mean, they love it there and I'm still getting the house in order here. Their rooms aren't finished. There'll be less upheaval for them – '

That was what I had thought. I listened for a moment as she tied herself into verbal knots trying to justify how much nicer and more convenient it would be for the children to spend their holidays in Wales and go back to school directly from there. She'd get down to see them, of course . . .

'Listen, Hazel – ' I interrupted her. 'I think it's time we had a little talk.'

'A talk? But we *are* talking – ' There was the sharp peal of a bell in the distance and a trace of genuine fear crept into her voice. 'Will you hold the line a minute, please? There's someone at the door – '

'Don't be frightened, Hazel,' I said. 'It's only Richard. Richard Sandgate. He volunteered to collect you and bring you over here.'

'At this hour?'

'Please come, Hazel. It really *is* a matter of life and death.'

'Is everything all right?' Lania was at the door as I hung up the phone. 'I saw Richard drive off. Has he – ? Is he . . . coming back?'

'You'd better come in.' I swung the door wide resignedly. 'He'll be back – and it's high time we all found out what's been going on.'

'Going on?' Lania followed me into the living-room. I saw her swift relieved glance at Richard's suitcase.

'This is nonsense, of course.' She took possession of the suitcase and began repacking it. 'Piers has left now and Richard is coming home with me. I'm sorry you've been troubled.'

'I think we'd better fold the sofa back into shape before they get here,' Arnold said. 'Can you help me, honey?'

'Before who get here?' Lania snapped the suitcase shut.

'Richard's picking up Hazel.' I helped Arnold get the sofa in order. 'We decided it's time for a showdown.'

'Hazel?' Lania was still caught up in her own

problems. 'What has she to do with all this?'

'Everything,' I said grimly.

We'd briefed Lania by the time Richard and Hazel arrived. She had been initially uncertain, but more than willing to admit that something strange might have been going on.

'John was always such a careful driver,' she remembered. 'I must admit, I did think it ironic that such a thing should have happened to him – of all people. In fact, I sometimes wondered – '

The doorbell rang and I left her in full flow of hindsight while I went to admit Hazel and Richard. They preceded me into the living-room. Richard seemed displeased, but not surprised, to find Lania there; Hazel just seemed numbed. I knew then that I was right.

'Sit down – ' I gestured her to a seat. She perched unhappily on the edge of a chair, looked around fearfully, and seemed relieved to find no strangers in the room.

'You could use a drink,' Arnold diagnosed, bringing her a large measure of the duty-free brandy we had picked up in Boulogne.

'Thank you.' She took it humbly and sat waiting for the blow to fall.

'I guess . . .' She smiled faintly. 'I guess perhaps I have.' Guilt shadowed her eyes. 'How did you find out?'

'It got to be obvious that something was wrong – ' I looked at her steadily – 'when somebody kept trying to murder Arnold.'

'Murder Arnold?' She paled. 'You can't mean it!'

'First, John Blake.' I underlined. 'Then, Arnold. And the only thing they had in common was that they'd both been putting in overtime being nice to you.'

'No!' I thought she was going to faint. 'No – that can't be true!'

'Can't it?'

'Then – ' She looked around wildly. 'Then – they've found me!'

'Who's found you?' Richard was shaken by the intensity of her emotion.

'Her husband and his friends,' I said. 'Remember that hostile character at the cocktail party?' I turned back to Hazel. 'Since you've got a husband jealous to the point of homicidal mania, didn't it ever occur to you that the least you could do was discourage the attentions of other men?'

'Oh, God!' she choked. 'If it were *only* that!' And burst into tears.

I stepped back, my bolt shot, and looked at her blankly. Arnold rushed forward and topped up her glass, although she'd scarcely taken a sip from it. Richard groped for a handkerchief and thrust it into her hand.

'Look, Hazel – ' She didn't look; she just kept sobbing into the handkerchief. I began to feel as though I were bullying a kitten, but I had to go on – for Arnold's sake. 'Hazel – '

'Actually – ' she raised her head – 'it's Mavis. My name is Mavis. It took me a long time to get used to Hazel, but now I can forget it again, can't I?'

'Mavis? . . . Hazel?' She'd lost me – or almost lost me. I looked at Richard. 'Then she isn't deaf, after all.' When she was off guard, she simply failed to respond to a name that was not really her own.

'I suppose there *are* children? Somewhere . . .?'

'Somewhere safe!' She glared at me defiantly. 'They changed schools – and I'll *never* tell you where they are. They've got to be kept out of this!'

'I wasn't planning to drag them in,' I assured her. 'I was just curious.'

'I've had enough of curiosity.' Her voice was flat. She dabbed at her eyes, but she had stopped crying. 'You don't know what it's like. Everyone staring . . . whispering . . . all the speculation. People thought I must have been involved, too. They wouldn't believe that I knew nothing about it. And then . . . the threats began . . .'

'So you got the children away to safety.' Bits of it were beginning to come clear.

'The police did.' Another piece clicked into place. 'They were . . . very good. Of course,' she smiled wanly, 'they've got it down to a fine art now. Terry wasn't the first . . . he won't be the last.'

'Terry, I take it, is your husband? And he's not a wildly jealous homicidal maniac?'

'Nothing of the sort! He's sweet and gentle – he'd never hurt anyone.'

'I take it he's not a Sales Director, either? He's not behind the Iron Curtain on an Export Drive? He's just behind the Iron Curtain.'

'He's not!' She was furious at the insinuation. 'He's only in prison. In this country. He was never a spy – he was only a . . . a Supergrass.'

'So that's it!' Richard whistled softly. 'Which trial

was it? One of the IRA ones, or – ' He broke off. 'Forgive me. I don't mean to pry.'

'Well, I *do*!' I wasn't going to be stopped by Richard's jolly old English reticence – which wasn't so evident when he decided he wanted a fight with his wife. 'I think we have a right to know. Damn it – somebody keeps trying to murder Arnold!'

'I'm afraid so,' she said. 'I'm terribly sorry about that.'

'*You're* sorry!' Arnold's sang-froid slipped.

'It was a . . . criminal case.' She found it easier to answer Richard. 'Terry got involved without realizing it at first. He was so pleased to get a job as Chief Accountant. But it was a dummy company, set up to . . . launder money from rackets and robberies. Even when he found out, it didn't seem too bad to go on working for them. He never knew the worst of the things they were doing – not until . . . the police arrested him.

'He wasn't wicked – even the police admitted that.' It was terribly important to her that we believe her. 'He was just weak. When the Fraud Squad swooped – they'd been investigating, gathering evidence, for a long time – he was horrified. He agreed to help them. He's a good, kind man, really – he just wanted to be able to buy nice things for me and the children – he'd never have hurt a fly.'

'So how come John Blake died?' I was sorry for her, but even sorrier for the innocent bystanders who had somehow got in the way of that great guy of hers.

'That wasn't Terry's fault! Not the way you mean it. After . . . after Terry testified, he knew the Directors would never forgive him. He helped the police trace a lot of the money, too. He . . . made it a condition that the police got his family away to safety. And they did. Rather, we thought they did – '

'His bosses put out a contract on Terry.' Richard supplied the only logical answer. 'Or am I wrong?'

'No . . .' She shook her head sadly. 'You're not wrong.'

'You seem to know a lot about it,' Arnold said to Richard, rather tactlessly.

'There have been so many cases reported over the past few years.' Richard shrugged. 'Inevitably, one has learned about such things.'

'Not nearly as much as I've learned.' Hazel was grim. 'The big men want revenge at any price. Even though they're behind bars, they manage to get word out. A contract on the Supergrass, open to anyone – and there are no end of takers. The money is good. The cheapest contract is five thousand pounds – it can go up to fifty thousand.'

Richard and Arnold both whistled. 'How much – ?' Arnold began, but even he realized that was too tactless.

'How much for Terry? It would be towards the upper end of the bracket. They hated him so much. The police expected the contract, they got me and the children away before the trial began. They gave me a new identity, sent the children to boarding school at the other end of the country, found this place for us to buy a house – ' Her voice broke. 'I've liked it here, I really have. I thought we could settle down and be happy here after Terry finished his sentence and joined me. We could have brought the children home then . . . once it seemed safe . . .'

'But it wasn't as safe as you thought,' I said. 'Someone had taken up the contract, found you and staked you out – waiting for your husband to turn up. Is that why John Blake was killed? Because he was mistaken for your husband?'

'I'm afraid so,' she said. 'Not that I realized it until now. I'd thought it was a genuine accident, although I still felt guilty because it wouldn't have happened if he hadn't been over that evening helping me.'

'Wait a minute – ' Arnold said. 'I thought your husband was still in prison. Why were they watching you? Why didn't one of the other prisoners kill him quietly and collect the money when he got out?'

'Oh, well . . .' She looked embarrassed. 'You see, Terry had been in protective custody for so long before the trial that it counted towards his sentence. Then there were all the usual remissions – '

'Quite often – ' Richard said coldly; the enormity of John's death was just coming home to him – '*too* often, these people are allowed out to visit their families. The law can be very grateful to a useful supergrass.'

Hazel winced. She hadn't missed the fact that she was becoming one of 'these people'. The pleasant respectable life she had yearned for was slipping away . . . again.

'If it's any comfort,' she said, 'it's quite probable that the person who killed John Blake has already been punished. Not for killing the wrong man, but because he might have drawn police attention to the contract by doing so. He might have alerted me, so that I moved away – perhaps to a place where I couldn't be found again. I – I wish I hadn't been so foolishly complacent. I suspected nothing.'

'And so they kept watching you, waiting for your husband to join you.' Richard was cold as a judge. 'Or visit you.'

'Actually, I've seen Terry several times – but never near here.' She seemed proud of having outwitted her enemies that much. 'The last time was in Boulogne.'

'The Invisible Man!' I exclaimed.

'What?' She was startled.

'That's where he comes in. He was there when the twins discovered you. A man in bandages.'

'Yes,' she said. 'I'll have to get used to the new face when the bandages come off. Terry had to have a bit of plastic surgery. It seemed safer – he had quite distinctive features.'

'Of course!' I said. 'Plastic surgery *had* to be part of the package. That was why they couldn't be sure which man was your husband. They didn't know what face he'd be wearing now.'

'You don't mean they thought *I* was her husband – ' Arnold was aghast. 'But I'm an American – and I've got the wife and kids to prove it. How could anybody have thought that?'

I narrowed my eyes and gave him a look he had no trouble interpreting as: *Because you've been snuggling up to her at every opportunity, the same way you wrapped yourself around that blonde at Pixie's New Year's Eve Party!*

'They're very suspicious – ' Hazel almost blushed. 'And you have no idea of the elaborate scenarios that are constructed to reunite husband and wife.'

'How could I fit into that kind of scenario?' Arnold asked incredulously. 'I've got a wife and kids of my own.'

'They might have thought the children were yours – ours – ' Hazel was growing embarrassed; she did not look at me. 'But they might have been very doubtful about the wife.'

'*What?*' Now *I* was incredulous.

'Well, you and Arnold *do* fight a lot, Nancy.' The stab in the back came from Lania, standing behind me. 'You know you're always nagging him – and in public, too.'

'You *were* shouting about divorce in the supermarket,' Hazel reminded me. 'Everyone heard you. My neighbour thought you meant it. It could have given anyone already suspicious the idea that you were . . . masquerading as his wife. No one would have been surprised if there had been one final public display – and then you returned to the States to get that divorce. Leaving Arnold – Terry – free to keep the children and move in with me.'

'I never thought of such a thing,' Arnold denied instantly. 'Besides, I'm *not* Terry. I'm Arnold Harper – and I can prove it.'

'The trouble is,' I told him, 'nobody ever asked you to prove anything. They were willing to kill you for yourself alone. For which, I would be the last to blame them – '

'You see?' Lania's voice soared triumphantly. She was enjoying herself for the first time in days. 'You're doing it again!'

'Look – ' I said. 'Isn't it about time we stopped

horsing around with side issues and called in the police?'

They all looked at me as though I'd suddenly grown a second head.

'Why?' Richard asked.

'What would you tell them?' Hazel wanted to know.

'The truth,' I said blankly. 'Somebody killed John Blake. Somebody's been trying to kill Arnold. Somebody should be arrested and put in jail.'

'But they *are* in jail,' Hazel said softly. 'The ones who are really guilty. The ones who put out the contract, although you could never prove it. And it would be almost impossible to discover the hit man who tried to kill Arnold. It might not even have been the same person each attempt.'

'There's not much that can be done,' Richard agreed.

'You mean my car's been sabotaged, I've been stabbed, kicked around, shoved under a bus – ' Arnold's voice rose – 'and I'm just supposed to shrug and forget it? John Q. Public gets screwed again!'

'That's what crime is all about,' Richard said. 'Us against them. All the grubby anonymous little chancers, striking in darkness and confusion and disappearing before they can be identified. Perhaps the only thing any of us can do is try to keep some order in our own lives and hope for the best.'

'I'm sorry.' Hazel choked back tears. 'I'd give anything if this hadn't happened – any of it!'

'It's not your fault,' I said. But it was. If she hadn't come to this town to start her new life, none of it would have happened. John Blake would still be alive and Rosemary's life unshattered. But Hazel – Mavis – was a victim, too.

'What will you do?' I asked softly.

'I'll let the police know my cover's blown. They'll have me out of here in a couple of hours.' She pushed herself slowly to her feet. She seemed to have aged ten years. 'Don't worry. After I've gone, they'll realize they were wrong again and Arnold will be all right.'

'But will you be all right?'

'Eventually, I suppose. It means we start all over again – ' She walked blindly towards the door. 'Another name, another town – perhaps even another country.'

'I'll drive you back,' Richard said.

'Do you think it's safe?' It slipped out; I could have bitten my tongue.

'I'll go with them,' Lania said quickly. 'It ought to be all right with another woman in the car.'

Richard looked at his wife thoughtfully. For a moment, I thought he'd refuse, then he nodded slowly.

'One other thing,' he said to Hazel. 'You'll need money and I gather you'll be leaving house and contents behind. I'd like to buy your living-room furniture. We need something comfortable and practical for ourselves – something the whole family can live in from now on.'

Hazel nodded.

Lania opened her mouth, shut it again, and lingered behind a moment as Richard and Hazel went out.

'The suitcase – ' she whispered to me. 'Just shove

it through the wall, would you? Then we needn't come back for it and disturb you.' She left hurriedly.

I stood looking at the suitcase. The wall – all the ramifications rose in my mind again. I still hadn't told Rosemary about that. The bedroom would have to be repapered – I hoped she hadn't been sentimentally attached to the old wallpaper. I'd have to get samples of wallpaper and send them over to her and let her choose. We'd probably have to repaint to match the new paper, too.

That was bad enough, but I *couldn't* tell her about Hazel. Nor could I tell her that John had been so uselessly, senselessly murdered. I'd write to Patrick and Celia; they could break it to her when they judged the time was right. Maybe they could let her enjoy the summer and tell her just before she was due to return to England. It might make it easier for her if she knew she'd never see Hazel again . . .

'You see, honey,' Arnold called me out of my reverie. 'Everybody's noticed it.'

'Noticed what?'

'You've got to admit it. Sometimes you treat me like a rat's ass.'

'Arnold, sometimes you *are* a rat's ass!'

'You're still mad about New Year's Eve, aren't you?'

'Mad enough.'

'But you're kinda glad they didn't manage to kill me, aren't you?'

'Glad enough . . .' I picked up the suitcase and started for the stairs. 'Coming?'

'I don't know. I was just thinking. That sofa looked pretty comfortable when it was pulled out. And it's quiet down here . . . and private. Why don't you get rid of that suitcase and come back down?'

'Hmmm,' I said. 'I'm not sure you deserve it but . . . maybe I will.'

A writers' colony's three cats—Had-I, But Known, and Roscoe—help out with the sleuthing in Marian Babson's comical, otherworldly mystery CANAPÉS FOR THE KITTIES. Turn the page for an exerpt . . .

1

CHAPTER TWENTY

Miss Petunia Pettifogg adjusted her gold-rimmed pince-nez and surveyed the tea table with deep satisfaction. 'I see that our invaluable Mrs Bloggs has outdone herself again,' she remarked to her sister.

'Jam sponge.' Lily began lifting the little white muslin tents covering the dishes to display the treasures hidden beneath. 'Scones, crumpets, walnut bread ... woman must have been baking all day.'

Miss Petunia closed her eyes briefly and inhaled the delicious fragrances. All part of the comfort and delight of coming home to their dear Blossom Cottage after a tedious and exhausting day in London trying to convince the singularly obtuse hierarchy at New Scotland Yard that there had, indeed, been yet another murder in the deceptively rural and peaceful village of St Waldemar Boniface.

'Let's eat,' Lily said, tilting the teapot and beginning to pour.

'But ... where's Marigold?' Miss Petunia looked around for her youngest sister.

'Off on some mysterious errand of her own,' Lily said. 'Don't know how long she'll be. No point waiting for her.'

Even as Lily spoke, they heard the sound of footsteps running down the path to Blossom Cottage and the quick scrape of a key in the lock. Then the front door slammed on loud and obnoxious shouting which came to them, unfortunately, all too clearly.

'Come back out here!' a male voice howled. 'And I'll *do* yer! Come out and I'll show yer what it's for!'

Another door slammed and Marigold was suddenly in the room with them, leaning against the door, her red-gold curls dancing, her bright blue eyes sparkling with the merriment of the chase.

'Oh, dear!' She tossed her head impishly. 'I'm rather afraid poor Colonel Battersby is *overrefreshed* again.'

'You mean the drunken sot is drunk again!' her sister Lily growled tigerishly. 'You must stop encouraging these vulgarians. One day you'll go too far.'

'I was merely following your instructions,' Marigold pouted. 'I was questioning him – very subtly – about the strange disappearance of his sister-in-law, the cyanide in his wife's cocoa, the bonfire which destroyed any evidence that might have been hidden in the compost pile and the reason why there were bloodstains on his knitted silk tie when, for no reason at all, he suddenly got very upset and began shouting at me.'

'So you came home immediately,' Miss Petunia said. 'How very sensible of you.' Outside, the shouting died to sporadic sulky outbursts.

'I most certainly did *not* desert my post that easily,' Marigold said indignantly. 'I went to the bar and bought him another drink. When I came back, he seemed quite reasonable and we had a pleasant little talk. He asked me how much I was insured for. Then, before I could answer, he said no matter how much it was, it wasn't enough.' She frowned thoughtfully. 'I hadn't realized that Colonel Battersby had taken to selling life insurance as a sideline.'

'He's sly, that man,' Lily growled. 'Sly and dangerous. As too many women in this village have found out . . . too late.'

'He's gone very quiet suddenly.' Miss Petunia felt a strange flutter of apprehension.

'Perhaps he's fallen asleep,' Marigold giggled.

'Passed out, you mean,' Lily said, lighting another cigarette.

'Oh, my dear, I wish you wouldn't.' Miss Petunia was moved to make one of her rare protests. 'You don't want to shorten your life.'

'Be quiet!' Lily ordered roughly.

'It's only for your own good, dear.' Miss Petunia was hurt.

'Not that, Pet –' Lily gestured towards the front of the house. 'I mean, listen . . .'

'Yes, I can hear something!' Marigold gasped, her eyes widening. 'It's the car! Of course, I took the keys away from him because he was in no fit condition to drive. That was when he got upset all over again. Then I threw the keys into the bushes when he was gaining on me, in order to distract him. He must have found them and gone back for the car. Oh, I hope he doesn't kill someone!'

'He's racing the motor,' Lily judged. 'He's heading this way –'

There was a tremendous crash at the front door.

'He's ram-raiding us!' Marigold shrieked.

'I'll put a stop to this!' Lily snarled. They all rushed out into the front hall.

The door was half off its hinges; the motor car blocked any hope of getting past it. As they stared aghast, it burst into flames.

'That does it!' Lily roared. 'The man is a menace and must be stopped. Marigold, ring the fire brigade. I'll take care of Colonel Battersby!' She led them into the front parlour and opened the window.

'Battersby, you old fool!' she bellowed. 'You're under arrest! This is a Citizen's Arrest! I demand that you step forward and surrender immed –'

The rock struck her on the temple with great force, hurling her back into the room where she lay motionless.

'Lily! Lily!' Miss Petunia knelt beside her. 'Speak to me!'

'Oh, Petunia –' Marigold put down the telephone, her hands shaking. 'There's no answer. There's not even a dial tone. Colonel Battersby must have cut the wires. The line is dead!'

'So is Lily,' Miss Petunia said grimly.

'What?' Marigold rushed over to stand beside her, looking down at her fallen sister. 'You can't mean it!'

'Thus was Goliath slain!' Miss Petunia rose to her feet, one hand clasping Marigold for support. Suddenly she felt quite giddy. 'Colonel Battersby has gone too far!'

'Oh, Petunia, what are you going to do?'

'Lily shall be avenged! Marigold, run upstairs and get me Daddy's old Service revolver. We have always kept it well cleaned and oiled in his memory. Now we are forced to take the law into our own hands!'

Marigold left the door ajar as she dashed from the room and Miss Petunia became aware of grey tendrils of smoke curling along the floor. As soon as she had dealt with Colonel Battersby, it might be wise to leave the cottage, as it seemed to be alight.

In the distance, she could hear Marigold coughing as she stumbled up the stairs.

'Be careful!' she called out instinctively. Marigold always dashed about so impetuously. Already she must have found the gun, for she was now hurrying back downstairs. The smoke was thicker.

Marigold must have been halfway down the stairs when there was a squeal and a shot rang out. There was the sound of a body – Marigold's body – falling down the stairs.

'Marigold!' Miss Petunia dashed into the front hall to find Marigold, as she had feared, lying at the foot of the stairs. Daddy's gun was still clasped to her bosom, above it a dark-red stain blossomed.

'Oh, Petunia,' Marigold said faintly. 'I tripped.' And said no more.

Tears, as well as smoke, blinding her eyes, Miss Petunia dragged Marigold's body into the parlour to lie beside Lily's. She could not bring herself to remove the gun from Marigold's hands.

She was alone now and must face her fate as best she might. The hallway, she had noticed, was alight at both ends. Colonel Battersby had obviously set another fire by the back door to trap them in the house.

There was only the window for escape. Coughing, she made her way to it. Strange, how difficult it was becoming to walk.

The window was still open, curtains fluttering in the breeze. Was that wise? Wasn't there something about not creating a draught in a house that was on fire? Perhaps she should close the window . . .

No! No! She must get out through the window. Laboriously, she threw one knee up on the sill and –

The rock crashed into her temple. Ah, but her head was harder than Lily's, she congratulated herself, even as she was being borne backwards by the force of the blow.

She fell across Lily and Marigold and rested on them a moment, fighting for breath. The room was completely fogged with smoke now. To think that she had reprimanded dear Lily for lighting a cigarette!

Smoke inhalation! She was being overcome by the smoke. Miss Petunia tried to push herself to her feet, even to her hands and knees, but she felt too giddy. She must try ... she must fight ... but ...

As she collapsed again across her sisters' bodies, the thought came to her that this really was ... *t*

h

e   *e n d*

Lorinda Lucas slid the last page out of her typewriter with a feeling of peace and accomplishment.

Quickly, she rolled another page into the machine. While the euphoria lasted, she could force herself to put the repellent Petunia, the nauseating Marigold and the appalling Lily through a few more of their paces. Paces which, unfortunately, would leave them triumphantly alive and kicking and ready to trudge through the next book in the series.

She typed steadily for another hour, then pushed her chair away from the desk. She stood and crossed to the dark-red filing cabinet where she hid her guilty secret, the death-dealing chapter, in the increasingly thickening folder marked 'FINAL CHAPTERS'. Soon she would have to begin another file folder – if she kept on like this.

And she probably would. Only to herself could she admit the deep satisfaction it gave her to dispose of the detestable Sibling Spinster Sleuths ('Try saying it quickly three times,' a critic had written. 'A few drinks may help, but you need a few drinks to pick up this sort of book in the first place.') in ever more lurid and gory detail. Other series writers might moan about how sick they were of their creations, but her own safety valve was blowing off steam quite nicely, thank you, as she wrote alternative endings for each book, each story and, sometimes, each idea. Reichenbach Falls had nothing on this!

As she turned away from the filing cabinet, the view from the window caught her eye. A picture-postcard village of quaint cottages, several with thatched roofs, sprawled into the distance along both sides of a winding road. Beyond it, a curving river sparkled in the fading sunlight. On the other side of her house, she knew, the view was of the High Street, which had several shops too many for a real village; the place had ideas above its station and was aspiring to Town status.

Lorinda made a face at the olde-worlde prettiness displayed below her and turned away, conscious of a dissatisfaction that was not solely caused by her professional discontent.

It had seemed like such a good idea at the time.

'I've made the discovery of a lifetime,' Dorian had brayed over the bridge table a year ago. 'Brimful Coffers. Delightful little village. Undiscovered, unspoiled, easy reach of London. Several highly desirable bijou residences going for a song because of the modernization they require. Cheap as they are, the natives can't afford 'em, but they'd just about come out of petty cash for *us* – and we'd always be sure of a fourth for bridge.'

Somehow, it had escaped her attention that she didn't care all that much for bridge. After living here for six months, she wasn't sure that she cared all that much for her colleagues, either.

Dorian King, as befitted the creator of Field Marshal Sir Oliver Aldershot, was a brilliant organizer. One by one, he had driven his chosen colleagues down to the village, introduced them to the local estate agent, accompanied them on their tours through the properties on offer, helpfully pointing out improvements that could be made . . . doing everything, in fact, except forcibly guiding their hands as they signed the contracts to purchase. Nor did he help with any mortgage arrangements, as it became clear to his victims that his idea of petty cash varied considerably from theirs.

Even so, it was, she had to admit, a lovely little cottage, and just what she had thought she wanted. Furthermore, the cats adored the garden and enjoyed exploring their immense new territory, revelling in a freedom that traffic had denied them heretofore. Another positive aspect was that there was no lack of cat-sitters or someone to pop in and feed them when she had to go up to town or off on a research trip. Nor did she mind being called upon in her turn to look after someone else's pet. No, the growing unease went deeper than that, but it was early days yet and no doubt they would all soon settle down satisfactorily.

Flip-flop . . . flip-flop . . . the familiar sound was followed by the thud of soft little paws on the stairs as the cats bounded up and headed unerringly for her study.

Had-I was in the lead, of course, with But-Known right behind her. They made a quick tour of inspection, then sat down side by side and regarded her with bright-eyed improbable innocence. She knew that look.

'*Now* what have you done?' She was instantly suspicious.

Flip-flap . . . flap . . . flap, scrabble . . . 'Aaarreeeooow . . .'

'Oh, not again!' she scolded.

'*Meerryooowrrr . . .*' The wail of distress soared upwards, filling the air, beginning to border on panic.

'All right, all right, I'm coming,' she called. The cats rose to their feet and followed her down the stairs. 'Let's go and see what the damage is,' she told them.

The huge orange cat was well and truly jammed into the catflap. Head and shoulders protruded, wriggling, with one trapped paw waving under his chin. He looked up piteously at Lorinda and renewed his struggles, but he could move no farther forward, nor could he back out.

'Oh, Pudding,' she said reproachfully. Pudding was not really his name, but it should be. He was sweet and thick. 'Will you never learn?'

'*Aaarrreeeooowww,*' he moaned, trying to twist around.

'No, no, don't do that. You'll only make it worse.' She stooped to pet him comfortingly. 'Just be calm and I'll get help.'

Had-I was going to be no help at all. Was she ever? With a disdainful look at the helpless captive, she strolled over to her bowl and ostentatiously began to munch.

'*Meeeyyyaaooo . . .*'

Had-I shot him a smug look and took another morsel, crunching it loudly. She was clearly saying, '*Yum-yum-yummy.*'

'You stop taunting the poor thing!' Lorinda pushed Had-I aside, scooped up a few of the tiny fish-shapes and carried them over to the catflap.

'Here . . .' She popped one into the eager mouth and then another. He was calming down now, with his mouth full and a trusted figure stroking his fevered brow.

'That's better.' Lorinda went to the telephone in the living room and pushed the automatic dialling button for one of the frequently called numbers. Then she held the receiver a safe distance from her ear, waiting for the shot that began the answer tape.

'BANG!! Ya missed me, sucker! You don't get Macho Magee that easy! I'm on the prowl down those mean streets with my trusty Roscoe, looking for trouble. Maybe I'll find it. If you want to find me, leave a message when the screaming dies . . .' A long shrill scream ended the announcement.

'You'd better come over here and pull out your trusty Roscoe,' Lorinda announced briskly. 'He's stuck in the catflap again.'

'They do it deliberately.' There was a click and the querulous voice began complaining. 'I've seen them. Those wretched creatures of yours lead my poor Roscoe on.'

It was too true to argue with. Had-I and But-Known all too clearly thought it was the best joke in town to lure poor Roscoe into their catflap and then laugh at him when he couldn't clear it and jammed halfway through.

'He ought to know better by now,' Lorinda said. 'But he's well stuck in this time and I'm afraid of hurting him.'

'Oh, all right. I'll be right there.' He slammed down the phone and Lorinda went back into the kitchen.

'All right, Roscoe,' she said carefully; she mustn't get caught calling him Pudding. 'Daddy's on the way.'

Still tranquillized by his snack, Roscoe regarded her amiably. But-Known, perhaps with a belated attack of conscience, was busily washing his face, which was also helping to soothe him. He had stopped struggling, but still looked terribly uncomfortable.

Had-I had abandoned her food bowl, finding no fun in it if Lorinda was going to be such a spoilsport as to share the munchies with Roscoe, and was perched on a chair watching the others. Now she lifted her head and turned towards the window, aware of an approaching presence before Lorinda could see or hear it.

It had to be Macho. Taking her cue, Lorinda gently eased the door open, trying not to panic Roscoe.

'Steady on, boy. It's all right. Don't worry.'

Reassurances were useless. Roscoe let out an unearthly shriek at discovering he was moving horizontally through the air at no volition of his own and without human arms around him.

'I'm coming! I'm coming, Roscoe!' The figure at the far end of the garden broke into a shambling run and lurched forward precipitously. 'Hang in there!'

Really, there wasn't much else Roscoe could do. He swung, suspended by his ample middle, from the catflap, hind legs scrabbling for purchase and yowled his terror to the skies.

'Here I am! Daddy's here!' Macho Magee dropped to his knees beside his anxious pet and glared up at Lorinda. 'I don't know why you have to have one of those porthole-type catflaps. It's antisocial!'

'It was here when I bought the house.' Lorinda sighed, they had been through this before. 'And my *own* cats,' she pointed out, 'have no trouble with it at all.'

'Nevertheless, the thing is a menace. You should take it out and replace it with a square flap with one end flush with the floor. That's the best kind. It's what I have.'

'It's draughtier,' she said, without adding that she did not particularly wish to allow Roscoe, however sweet he might be, unlimited access to her house. Nor did she think Had-I and But-Known would appreciate an interloper roaming through their territory at will, however well they got on with him.

Roscoe had begun purring trustfully and Macho Magee got to his feet to assess the problem.

'It looks pretty bad this time,' he said fretfully, glaring at Lorinda as though it were her fault. 'We may have to dismantle the flap.'

'No,' Lorinda said.

'Mmmm . . .' He walked around the door, checking both ends of his cat. 'Perhaps, if we grease him . . .'

'We did that last time and he didn't like it.'

'True, and it took him days to get all the butter out of his fur.' Macho took another turn around the door. Roscoe was beginning to look anxious again.

'If you can work that paw loose from under his chin,' Lorinda suggested, 'you ought to be able to back him out then.'

Had-I and But-Known just sat there and looked superior, quite as though they'd had nothing to do with luring Roscoe to his entrapment.

'I don't know . . .' Macho knelt before his cat again and gently took hold of the paw. 'Easy now . . .' he soothed. 'Easy . . . does it . . .'

If his fans could see him now . . . Lorinda thought, not for the first time. She looked down on the polished pink dome of the creator of the eponymous Macho Magee, arguably the hardest-boiled private eye in print; certainly the most politically incorrect. What Macho Magee hadn't blackmailed, stabbed, strangled, set alight or blown away wasn't worth thinking about. He considered any book that didn't attract a minimum of fifty letters of complaint one that hadn't come up to scratch. The man's very name was a challenge. Deliberately so.

It had to be. His real name was Lancelot Dalrymple, a good enough name in ordinary life, but not one to stir the blood or set the cash registers jingling in the private-eye world, although it might do well in the realm of gardening books. A Dalrymple sounded as though he would be more at home mulching roses and bedding begonias rather than every tough blonde who strayed across his path.

'There, we've got it now.' He freed the paw, easing it through to the other side of the porthole. Roscoe immediately lunged forward, trying to get into the room with them.

'No, no, Roscoe.' Macho restrained him. 'Just cup his head in your hands, will you?' he instructed Lorinda. 'I'll go round and pull and you guide his head through. Mind that he doesn't catch his ears.'

Lorinda crouched and encircled Roscoe's head, murmuring softly to soothe him as he began moving backwards, his eyes rolling wildly.

'Nearly there . . .' She protected his ears as his head vanished through the opening and the flap fell back into place.

'That's better. You're all right now.' Roscoe reappeared, cradled in Macho's arms and Lorinda swung the door shut behind them.

'Come and have a drink,' she invited. 'You're through for the day now, aren't you?'

'I might do a bit more later but, basically, yes.' He carried Roscoe into the living room and settled in an armchair. Had-I and But-Known trailed along in his wake, eyeing Roscoe thoughtfully.

The fictional Macho Magee drank nothing but the genuine Mexican tequila with the worm curled at the bottom of the bottle (often the closest he got to ingesting any protein in the course of an entire book). Fortunately, Lancelot Dalrymple was quite content with a dry sherry. Lorinda poured sherries for both of them and set a bowl of mixed nuts within easy reaching distance.

Had-I and But-Known moved forward to investigate the bowl and retreated, flinging Lorinda looks of utter disgust. No cheese! No pâté! What was hospitality in this house coming to? They sat down together and concentrated their attention on Roscoe again.

Roscoe stirred restively in his owner's arms.

'No, no, stay here.' Macho tightened his grip. 'Ignore them. You know they only lead you into trouble. Treacherous jades!'

His language might also surprise his fans, as would the Byronesque ponytail tied with a black velvet ribbon trailing down to his shoulders. Both were probably a legacy of his years as a history teacher and his abiding interest in the subject.

'Book going well?' Ignoring his opinion of her cats (her own opinion of his wasn't all that high), Lorinda sank into the facing armchair and leaned back.

'Oh, well enough.' Now it was Macho who appeared restive. 'I need to get the body count higher, but I should be able to take care of that in the next chapter.'

'I'm sure you'll manage it,' Lorinda agreed absently. She was mentally composing and discarding opening sentences, trying to find a subtle lead-in to the subject she wished to introduce.

'I suppose you've heard the latest?' Macho had no such inhibitions. He leaned forward intently, loosening his hold on Roscoe, who promptly slid to the floor and ambled over to join Had-I and But-Known.

'Which latest?' The way gossip was proliferating in this village, there was a multiple choice.

'They've rented the last of the flats in Coffers Court. And guess who's got it?'

'Mmmm . . .' Macho was looking entirely too gleeful. 'Why do I get the feeling I'm not going to like the answer?'

'Because you're not. Go ahead.' He tugged at his goatee, pulling down his lower lip and disclosing a set of thin gnarled lower teeth. 'Who's the last creature in the world you would care to tiptoe hand-in-hand into the sunset with?'

At the moment, Macho himself was becoming the leading contender in that category. Lorinda regarded him without fondness.

'There are so many,' she murmured. And most of them seemed to be congregating in Brimful Coffers.

'The absolute worst,' he insisted. 'Beside whom the Marquis de Sade looks like St Francis of Assisi.'

'No!' Lorinda leaped to her feet. Had-I and But-Known had closed in on either side of Roscoe and were hustling him towards the kitchen. 'Come back here! You're not going to jump him through the catflap again!'

They stopped short and gave her injured looks. How could she think such a thing of them?

'Just a minute, Macho.' She hurried into the kitchen and turned the knob immobilizing the catflap. They could butt their heads against it in vain now.

'Roscoe! Come here, Roscoe!' Macho appeared in the doorway and advanced on his pet.

Roscoe evaded the outstretched arms and strolled over to the bowl of dry cat food and began to help himself. Had-I gave Lorinda a reproving look for spoiling all their fun and sat down and began to wash her face. But-Known went over to stand hopefully in front of the fridge.

'They're all right now,' Lorinda said. 'Come and finish your drink.'

'I don't know.' Macho settled back in his chair and allowed Lorinda to replenish his drink. 'Sometimes I think I should just get myself a tank of goldfish.'

'Not while Roscoe is still around,' Lorinda said.

'No, no. They wouldn't last ten minutes.' Macho was instantly cheered by the thought of his pet's hunting prowess. 'I only hope he never gets a chance at Dorian's tank of tropical fish.'

'Amen, amen,' Lorinda said fervently. The mere thought of Had-I and But-Known getting within paw-dipping distance of Dorian's aquarium was enough to make her feel faint.

'Cold fish,' Macho mused. 'Dorian, I mean. It quite amazed me when he began lobbying for all of us to come and occupy the same village. He's the last person in the world I would have suspected of having any desire for the company of his colleagues – on a long-term basis, that is.'

'Plantagenet!' Lorinda suddenly made the connection with Macho's earlier teasing. 'Plantagenet Sutton! Tell me it isn't true!'

'True enough,' he sighed. 'Pity. Coffers Court must have been quite a respectable place when it was occupied by flint-hearted bank managers foreclosing on widows and orphans.'

'How true,' Lorinda agreed.

The decommissioned bank building had been designed with typical late-Victorian lavishness to resemble a wealthy land-owner's town house rather than a commercial establishment. Built of sandstone, now weathered to a rich gold, festooned with window boxes filled with seasonal blooms, it dominated one corner of the village green. Since the architect had been in the forefront of the technology of his time, along with the obligatory marble hall, it boasted a luxurious red-plush-and-mirrored lift with a padded bench curved invitingly around the walls. Thus patrons could be conveyed in solid comfort from the bank manager's office on the top floor to deposit their valu ables in the basement vault. The vault had now been divided into a caretaker's flat and a series of boxrooms providing storage for the tenants of the other flats.

It was a beautiful building and had been transformed into a dream block of flats. Too bad about the people in it.

'The neighbourhood is really going down,' Macho said. 'I hadn't thought it could sink any lower after Gemma Duquette moved in – but now this!'

'Plantagenet Sutton,' Lorinda mourned. 'Are you absolutely sure?'

'Ground-floor left-hand flat.' Macho was certain of his facts. 'I saw the furniture being moved in this morning. No one could mistake that wing chair and lamp table. No one in the business, that is It's practically his logo.'

'That's pretty conclusive. She hadn't really doubted him; Macho was an expert gossip. Probably they all were. Keeping tabs on friends and neighbours could be looked on as an exten sion of their work. What was a book, after all, but the retailing of the alarms, excursions and minutiae of everyday life until it reached a conclusion tidier than any life usually provided? Did they become writers because they were so very interested in gossip? Or did being writers make them preternaturally inter-ested in gossip?

Had-I and But-Known sauntered in and leaped up to sprawl out, one on each arm of Lorinda's chair. She stroked them absently. Roscoe followed and leaped up on Macho's lap. A faint concerted purr began to thrum as background music to their conversation. Outside, dusk began to settle over the village. It was all so comfortable and companionable ... but for how much longer?

Plantagenet Sutton had come to live in their midst. Life could never be the same again.

CANAPÉS FOR THE KITTIES
by Marian Babson—
A delightful mystery now available in
hardcover from St. Martin's Press!

Bettina Bilby has agreed to board her neighbors' felines for a long holiday weekend: an expectant tabby, a pampered blue-eyed Balinese, a depressed ginger Persian with a cod-liver-oil addiction, and Adolf, an imperious mouser with a patchwork face.

But during a freak storm, a carrier pigeon is downed on the doorstep with a tiny load of large flawless diamonds. And Bettina's dilemma escalates as Adolf gobbles up one of the gems and a succession of elegant but shifty strangers prowl the gardens, offending the cats, and bringing in their wake back-door bloodshed and murder.

THE
DIAMOND
CAT

MARIAN BABSON

THE DIAMOND CAT
Marian Babson
_____ 95660-6 $5.50 U.S.